By Any
And
All Means

BY: KAREN PIVOTT

www.amazon.com/author/karenpivott

BY THE SAME AUTHOR
BOOKS ON KINDLE and IN PRINT
NON FICTION
Airbags and Starting Over
Back On the Road Again
Always Travel With Your Basket
CHILDRENS FICTION
Birthdays at the Bay
Royce and Billy
FICTION
By Any Other Circumstances
By Any And All Means

FOREWORD

Jenna a woman now well into her middle years has not only learned many of life's lessons, she has also learned the value of them. This puts Jenna in a place of freedom of sorts where she is able to make better decisions for herself.

Life being life it also means Jenna reads the world around her better, and is able to be a positive support for those people who come into her life.

Jenna is also finding that when you think you can retire from life, life may present you with other opportunities and rather than slow down you just may need to shift a gear or two...

Disclaimer

This is a work of fiction. Names, characters, businesses, places, events and incidents are either the product of the author's imagination or used in a fictitious manner. Any resemblance to actual persons, living or dead, or actual events is purely coincidental

CONTENTS

BY ANY AND ALL MEANS

Acknowledgement

With thanks and love always to my husband
Alan.

CHAPTER ONE

Jenna had been away from her home for what seemed like a very long time. It wasn't of course. In truth Jenna conceded it was a very long time collectively, but lots of smaller trips in actuality.

Jenna had been to Australia to stay with family in two states for a month each time. Came home then unexpectedly she received tickets to visit family in Canada for four weeks, this trip meant Jenna was travelling almost back to back, so she immediately extended her mail being collected at the post office. A trip to the local travel agent followed the phone call, and her travel agent Amanda who as always was pleased to see Jenna back safely, was visibly bemused that Jenna was finding herself unpacking, repacking and on another stay away. Given she was going to Canada this allowed Jenna to arrange a stopover to see Jason in America whom she supported, on her way home. Jason was doing very well with his studies there. The stopover due to one thing and another became a stay of more than a week at no additional cost to her which was all the better.

If Jenna had been a woman who believed in coincidence then that is what she would have put the extended stay down to, but Jenna was not such a person. Life had taught her that everything without exception happens for a reason, as was the case this time.

Jason was doing well with his studies. He was missing home. Jason's mother had received a promotion at her work which meant she had to postpone her arranged trip. Changes in the following year's tuition had also occurred so Jenna found herself in the right place,

at the right time for Jason, and became
his mother by proxy as Jason put it.
Jenna reflected on the timing, the airline's
technical difficulties. The unseasonal
weather. How opportune it all had been
and of course it had all worked out
perfectly.

Sitting at her dining room table with
a cup of black tea she looked at her
suitcases, the dust on her china cabinet,
smelled the stale odour of a house that
has been shut up, and said out loud. "Yes
it really is good to be home, even though
the chores need doing, and of course I will
have to get some milk and food in." It was
a statement to the house more than
anything, to let it know she was once
again in residence.

The thing about staying with family
and friends she mused is,   when you say
something, someone generally answers
you back, or responds in some way. You
can get used to that rather quickly. With
that thought she put her now empty cup
into the sink and made her way to bed.

Jenna woke late the next morning to
the sound of rain. Rising slowly she
walked to the window, pulled back the
drape and raised the cedar venetian blind

expecting to see the green paddock which bordered her property, instead there was a rather large bulldozer parked in front of her, with a man climbing aboard it. He waved and the next minute the machine roared into life.

"Well if I had wanted to go back to bed for more sleep there really isn't any point in that now." Jenna had spoken and made her way to the bathroom to get ready for the day.

Finding her rice crackers and spread where she had left them before embarking on her travels clearly labeled. "First breakfast on your return." Jenna made herself breakfast, boiled the jug and made herself a cup of berry tea then strolled to her letterbox. The mail was there to greet her. There were two bundles and each bundle was held together by two rubber bands. Making her way back to the house she ate her crackers, sipped her tea and began sorting through her mail. There were the bills which had been prepaid before her departure on her travels so they were a mix of bills due, payments made and statements of balances owing. To Jenna's surprise things were still in credit so that was a nice surprise to come home to.

There was a letter from her editor asking her to consider writing just one more book, and then there was a letter from the local council. Jenna thought this was odd as she had paid her rates bill and the rates weren't due for another two months yet. She opened the letter to find it was a notification that the land adjoining her property was to be developed for residential use and any objections were to be submitted to the Council by September 16. Now November Jenna realised that whatever the submissions were had not slowed the development so there it was, the realisation that her view of green paddocks was no longer going to be hers. Not such a great welcome home on that front then.

Putting that letter to one side Jenna continued sorting the mail and found there were several letters from the Council on this matter, and today it seemed was the ground breaking day of the newly approved residential development which was to neighbour her property from now on. There was notification also of dust and noise being present and the process

by which existing residents could notify
Council if these became excessive.

Jenna smiled then shook her head.
"Summer is knocking on our door so of
course it will be dusty. Excessive dust.
How does one measure that I wonder?
Noise yes well that is measureable.
Progress and change bring with them all
manner of extras as we know." Jenna said
walking passed her wooden hat sitting
proudly on her wall.

Gathering her handbag, checking
she had her license, and putting on a light
cardigan Jenna made her way through to
her garage and got into her car, checking
her rain jacket was on the front seat where
she usually had it in case she had to go
out in the rain and yes it was there, the
remote opened the door, Jenna turned the
key and the car's motor turned over and
the engine began running.

"Let's go shopping." Jenna said and
drove out of the garage closing the garage
door behind her.

As she neared the shops the rain
eased, and Jenna found a park right
outside the supermarket next to the
Disability Parking space. This suited
Jenna because, Jenna had worked out

some time ago that those parks, are just a bit wider giving you more room to manouvre your trolley.

The one thing that Jenna found the true confirmer of your arrival home was the supermarket. The layout was the same. There were always specials. Some things had increased in price and the smells and busyness of the place was familiar and comforting at the same time. The delicatessen offered a wide variety of goods, and with Jenna just back and the day disappearing so quickly she chose to purchase cold cuts of meat, and salads for her immediate dinner with the expectation that she would have some for her lunch the next day.

It always surprised Jenna that no matter how much or how little there was on your grocery list, you seemed to spend about the same amount of time in the supermarket, usually an hour on average, unless of course you came across people you knew who stopped for a chat, and Jenna found herself being greeted by many people today. Everyone had an opinion on the new development, but alas no one it seemed had put in any submissions, and when Jenna was asked why she hadn't, she had to remind people she had been away. It seemed that not everyone, in fact very few people were happy about more building going onto what had been productive farm land over many generations, but then the current generation it seemed had lived beyond their means on the property, and with the falling of milk powder prices globally, they had found themselves with an unsustainable level of debt to service, so selling the land was the option they went with. "The bank, the developer and the people who sold them their new house two towns away were all very happy. " As Mrs. Hazlett said standing in front of the shelf stocked with Baked Beans. "I am quite sure they are very happy to have moved out before the dust and the noise invade our town and ruin our summer."

Jenna found this very amusing and tried to stifle a smile because Mrs. Hazlett lived on the other side of the town and would be nowhere near either the dust, or the noise.

CHAPTER TWO

Due to the feelings expressed to her, and her proximity to the Council Jenna decided to go in and ask what the procedure was if residents found themselves inundated with both, excessive noise and dust.

Sally was on the desk and gave Jenna a big smile with a "Welcome back. How was Jason?"

"Thank you Sally. Jason is fine and has told me to say hello to you as well. Sally I am here to find out what I do if the noise and dust becomes excessive with the activity that is taking place on my back boundary."

"Yes it is going to be noisy and dusty and I have a pamphlet here explaining the procedure, but over Christmas we are asking people to be patient as we will be on skeleton staff."

"Sally are the developers on skeleton staff?"

"Sadly no. Look Jenna just between us there are a lot of unhappy people in the town about this, but it is going ahead. Can you stay with someone while the development stage is in progress?"

"Sally I just returned home, and no my family now all live overseas."

Jenna was not angry with Sally. Jenna was however becoming quite suspicious about the whole timing of the development and decided to look into who was in charge of the development of the acres no hectares she gave herself a mental reminder, of land behind her. Information was scant at best and something just did not feel quite right. Jenna couldn't put her finger on it, but she was definitely going to be actively seeking information over the coming days. Jenna would be Skyping her family in a couple of days and decided she would ask her son David if he had heard anything from any of his former neighbours on the new subdivision. With this thought Jenna began her journey home to unpack her groceries, then unpack her suitcases. It will be dinner then bed again in no time she assured herself. I will phone a few of the neighbours tomorrow she decided as she put the last bag of groceries into her kitchen.

Jenna kept herself busy over the coming days attending to household and garden chores. The agreed time for the Skype call to her family in Australia came about much more quickly than she thought it would. As agreed David spoke last. The family of course were all missing her after her stay, and were arranging her trip the following year. This was all news to Jenna of course. Jenna was still recovering from the trips she had taken in this current year.

David took over the chair, "Good to see you mum, I am pleased we have that chit chat out of the way, before we talk about your development, I would just like to say I miss you as well."

"Thank you David. Things have been a little Hurley Burly shall we say with my additional travel to your brother's in Canada and I find myself missing you all as well. I am pleased that I have stayed with you all though. Your sister was very good to have arranged my stay with them first of course. As Richard said someone has to be first maybe it will be us next year that you stay with first. Now tell me, what have you heard over there from your neighbours here?"

"I have been talking to Sam from across the road in the house with the very bright red roof.

"Oh yes Sam the builder. Why didn't I think to call him?"

"In all fairness mum, why would you? It is not like you know him, anyway he agrees that everything happened very quickly. By very quickly he said and I quote "much more quickly than anything else has ever happened", so he has the feeling that it is a done deal. What he has suggested is that the residents go back to Council with a proposal that accommodation is provided away from the noise and dust if that becomes excessive."

"What are the actual chances of Council agreeing to that?"

"Probably not great. It will however keep the dialogue going."

"So the rumour that this is a done deal is correct."

"Yes mum that does seem to be the case. You are welcome to spend Christmas here with us if you're not travelled out that is?"

"Thank you David but I really need to spend time here. If the worst happens and I am dusted and noised out I will spend some time in the far north. It has been years since I was up there. I am quite sure there will be the odd vacancy available at a motel or something which is not an option other people may have."

"Nothing changes does it mum you always look at the positive."

"Well it took me a long time to get to the positive so it is always relative to me, and with the building going on it does seem to be even more relative in a time sensitive way. I love you and miss you David how about we Skype again next Thursday say 8 o'clock your time?"

"Are you sure that's not too late for you?"

"Not Thursday. I have been asked by Reverend Nicholls to address a group of young women about creative writing. This of course David is one of life's ironies. In the beginning I couldn't cut it as a creative writer so I resorted to publishing books involving recipes and everyday happenings in our community. Just short articles to start with of course. Let me just say this is one of the character building episodes that keep popping up in my life."

"Now mum you are always saying it's never too late to try something new."

"Trust you to remember that. Have a great week. Talk soon."

Jenna pressed the little red phone icon on her end and just like that they were gone. As fast as the green paddock on her boundary had been gone. Her view was one of brown dirt already. I wonder she thought, who could get a consent and get started so quickly. In not one of the pieces of written correspondence she had opened, had it said what the residential development was.

"First thing tomorrow morning I will ring young Sally and ask her what the development is." Jenna said to space she occupied and looked at her Kauri hat as if it concurred with her intention.

The noise woke her promptly at seven the next morning. Rolling over she looked at her clock and felt quite defeated before she had even put her feet on the floor.

"What's the point of even setting an alarm clock?" She said and got out of bed.

Looking out her window she decided the noise was just one companion she would have to learn to live with. The window sills were moving to the vibration of the diggers and other excavation vehicles now moving as one preparing the ground for its next adventure.

Jenna went to the kitchen and put the jug on so she could make herself a cup of tea and while the water was heating she got herself presentable for the day and the world at large.

The paper had arrived at the front door so Jenna picked it up and sat at the dining room table and began reading the article on the front page.

"Ground broken-International consortium to build retirement village for 200... " The article began. Residents of a small rural town ...... Jenna read the article and rose to make herself her first cup of tea for the day. Looking out of her kitchen window, while her tea brewed, she realised that the trench which was being dug was to house a new concrete wall, and that she would have absolutely no rural outlook now at all. Unexpectedly she felt quite sad, but she felt even sadder, for the family who over the generations had been good stewards of the land, and preserved it for the following generation to sustain them.

"Yes." she said "We live in an 'I want it now society' but that society is rendering our communities unrecognisable it would seem."' Jenna's thoughts were interrupted by the phone ringing, and as she picked up the phone she heard, "Jenna is that you? Of course it is. It's Jean Hazlett. Have you seen the paper? Well I am just ringing to let you know we are going away and you are most welcome to have the use of our place if you like. I know we can't give you your little piece of paradise back now that you find yourself in suburbia rather than in the country so to speak, but rest assured whatever we can do to make it easier for you please don't hesitate to ask."

"Well Jean. I am really at a loss for words."

"Oh dear" said Jean with a bit of a giggle "that really is not good for a writer now is it?"

"No. Not even a retired writer. I have to confess this whole business is quite something. Well what can I say? It is happening there's absolutely no doubt about that. I have the noise, the dust, and the smell to prove it, not to mention the view."

"Yes quite. I will see you at Church on Thursday night I am making the tea and putting out the supper. Talk then? "and with that the phone line was dead and Jean was gone.

Jenna didn't know what was the bigger surprise, the offer or the phone call itself. Of all the people Jenna knew Jean was not a person she would ever have thought of as a person who would offer practical assistance in such a perfunctory manner. One of life's surprises. As with life's ironies the timing is always perfect and none of it is coincidental. Jenna of course did not believe in coincidence and never had. Things happen for a reason she chastised herself in her thoughts. Good will come from it. Not right this minute for me but for two hundred people and staff members very probably coming from our community the development can't be built quick enough.

Progress yes David was all about progress he would see this as a good thing.

KAREN PIVOTT

CHAPTER THREE

Jenna was at her desk and right on cue the familiar sound of the skype ring entered into the vacuum of silence waiting for its arrival. With the click of an icon David's smiling face was looking at her.

"Yes. Hello mum. I hear your neighbours are to grow to 200. That's progress for you."

"It most certainly is progress for the 200, the staff, and the shareholders, but I am not so sure about me?"

"What happened to the optimist?" David said.

"The optimist is still in there, I am just finding her hard to locate at the moment."

"In all seriousness mum what are you going to do if anything?"

"At this stage the Hazlett's have offered me the use of their home over the Christmas period while they are away."

"Jean Hazlett?"

"You look as surprised as I must have sounded when she phoned me to make the offer. How did you find out so soon?"

"Sam. He phoned me to bring me up to speed. It has to be one of the best kept secrets of the town. He tells me that apparently this has been in the wind for quite some time, but the Council was working on it quietly in case it fell over. The two previous developments never materialised so they were being cautious. Once the money was finalised voila consent process began, meetings, approvals and now."

"Action as they say before the camera rolls. My next new view will be a concrete fence. I have been checking out some outdoor wall art so all is not lost."

"Are you sorry you moved from the large sprawling villa?"

"No not at all. I will be staying put for the time being everything else is working well for me, and Jean understands that. She is quite cross

about the whole thing, and they live so far
away from it all being across town.”

“Yes. I have been thinking about
that. Four years ago there was to be a
new motel on their side of the town and
the neighbours got very vocal about it.”

“Oh yes. I do remember that.”

“Well the developer was Jean’s son.”

“Jean and her husband don’t have
any children.” Jenna replied.

“Jean and her first husband had a
son. Sam is related to Jean. The son was
raised by his grandparents. His father’s
parents. Jean was grief stricken and did
not cope well with the loss of her husband
at the time. Her son came back into her
life as an adult. Sam said she tried to
help him with the development but council
withheld consent.”

“But that developer died of a heart
attack.”

“Yes mum. Just like his father.
They were both twenty eight.”

“Well I never. I had no idea. I have
known Jean for…Well it doesn’t bear
thinking about. Anyway the ground is
being worked well so things have well and
truly started, although I think I will stay
put. Having said that though I actually

don't feel that I will be here for much longer which is odd."

"I am sure you will be fine with your neighbours once the noise and dust have settled that is. I must go."

And with that the screen went blank and Jenna was once again surrounded by the symphony of silence she knew only too well and had a much better appreciation for these days.

The following morning Jenna woke to her alarm clock which was a surprise. As big a surprise as the silence that greeted her ears and the lack of action across her back boundary when she moved her drapes off the window.

"Looks like we are having a quiet day today." She informed the house and got on with her day without another thought about it.

The day ran very smoothly for Jenna she got household chores done. Called in to see her neighbour Geraldine who had been affectionately called Ginny in her younger days, but now preferred the stature her full first name afforded her. Geraldine had just returned from her holiday with family overseas something she and Jenna had in common that year.

She and Jenna had a great catch up over Devonshire tea.

Geraldine was as shocked to find how much things had changed as Jenna had been, but for Geraldine the word or concept of progress was not in her dialogue at all. Geraldine was very vocal about it, and had lots to say, as Jenna had expected, but resigned herself to the situation as one she could resolve only by shifting which she informed Jenna she would be making enquiries about forthwith.

"Well when I say forthwith of course I mean in the new year. Then again if I wait until the development is finished perhaps I could shift into there. What do you think about that Jenna?"

"I think you will do what you think is best for you when you have time to think all your options through. If you are serious about shifting into the Retirement Village then perhaps you had better enquire about availability."

"Really? It hasn't even been built yet."

"The reason it is being built Geraldine is because there is a need for it. You know what they say it is all about."

"Supply and demand. Yes. Didn't we get that thrown down our throats in the eighties and nineties?   Jenna I am coming up to eighty and the family have been making suggestions in this area. "Don't mention the Rest Home subject you know the Forbidden Subject." I overheard one of the grandchildren saying when they were all assembled in the kitchen clearing up after dinner one night. My grandchildren in their thirties now I might say, and they refer to a Retirement Village option as the Forbidden Subject. Am I that out of kilter with what needs to happen for me?"

"The thing about age Geraldine is this" Jenna began," when you are thirty you think you have your whole life in front of you. You forget that a third has gone by already, and that some of your friends may have used up their life and passed over before they were even thirty. Thirty is such a busy time. Work, family."

"If only there was some more family. They seem to leave it very late to start a family these days. Things have changed."

"Not really. People are able to make different choices and decisions to us

Geraldine, because they are living in a different time to us."

"Jenna you are a good twenty plus years younger than me."

"I know but we share a generation."

"Do you know I never thought about it in that way? I hope that doesn't mean you are thinking of shifting into the retirement Village."

"Not quite yet." Jenna said, and with that she left Geraldine for her afternoon nap.

It was such a lovely afternoon. Not too hot so Jenna decided to walk to the town boundary, then back home again to enjoy some fresh air and stretch her legs. It was much easier to do this now because there was a foot path provided, where before there was only the road verge. Taking in the sights as she walked and listening to music on the mp3 player her grand-daughter Deanna had given her before she migrated to Australia, Jenna became quite lost in her own thoughts, until she spotted something just ahead, and to the left of the foot path.

Jenna instinctively turned her mp3 player down, and moved with cautious resolve towards the protruding object with

a somewhat sinking feeling in her
stomach, which became heavier the closer
she got. There just behind the small
shrubbery was a man. He was very still.
His clothing was dishevelled and there was
blood by his right shoulder. The man was
lying face down. Jenna crouched down
and felt for a pulse on his right wrist, but
there was nothing. His wrist, and arm
were completely lifeless. Jenna rose
slowly and took out her cell phone, dialled
111, gave details, explaining that she had
found a dead man and their location to the
woman on the end of the phone, and
waited as she was directed to do so for the
Police to arrive.

Jenna stepped quite some distance
away from the man and said to the man,
"I didn't see that coming, but I wonder if
you did? "

The thing about waiting for an
arrival is that time seems to slow. It
doesn't of course, but there is so much
that goes on in your mind when you come
across the unexpected, the tragic, any and
all manner of things really, and when you
have done what you are supposed to and
then you are told to wait it is almost like
an anti-climax. You are parked Jenna

thought. When her children were born she reflected that her husband had said as much to her "It is all right for you because you are having the baby. Me I have to just wait."

How odd Jenna thought she hadn't thought about Adam for quite some time, and with those few words a memory had been triggered. Her thoughts were interrupted by the sound of a siren. Jenna looked down at her cell phone it had been seven minutes since she had called. Who would have thought seven minutes could feel so long. Looking over at the police car Jenna was delighted to see that Mark Denton was on duty.

"Can I call someone for you?"

"Thank you Mark but no. I have had time to collect myself. I have felt for a pulse on his right wrist which involved moving his arm to ascertain which service to ask for when I rang 111, but I haven't touched anything else. There is a wallet further to the right I think. It may not be a wallet but it looks like one."

"Jenna I am so sorry you have come across this."

"Better me than a child though Mark. Has anyone been reported missing?"

"Have you seen anyone suspicious in the area Jenna?"

"No. The truth is I haven't been back long. There are so many new people with the development happening, and the farming boom. I mean there are new people, but who is to say they are suspicious."

"What were you doing here?"

"Me. Oh I was just going for a walk to the town boundary. Stretching my legs. I had been to see Geraldine. Geraldine Walker. Two doors down from me."

"I can hear my colleagues are coming. Jenna do you mind sitting in the Police car. You are quite pale. I think I will get the ambulance to come and we will get you checked. This will have been quite a shock for you."

"I will sit in your Police car, but don't trouble yourself for an ambulance. I have had a bit of a shock but I am all right. The Coroner is the one you will need to be calling. I see you have been promoted to Sergeant. Congratulations. Now you just get on with whatever else you have to do. Secure the scene and so on." Jenna said as she made her way to the Police car. Once seated she was very pleased Mark had suggested it because she was beginning to feel quite wobbly. The young Constable who was with Sergeant Mark Denton came to the car and handed her a blanket. She wrapped it around herself and waited. This round of waiting was quite different. Time just seemed to blur as Jenna was surrounded by movement, people, activity and the temperature dropping as the day went on.

There were more questions and Jenna was driven home, and given a card to say she would be contacted by Victim Support. Once inside her home Jenna went to the phone and rang Jean Hazlett. Jean and her husband seemed to appear like magic and they had hot food with them. Jenna was in quite a dazed state when they arrived and Jean immediately set about making a pot of tea and looking for a bottle of something.

"Roy can you bring me the Brandy please." she asked as she reached for cups, plates and found the cutlery.

"You may not feel like it but you having a Brandy, food and a cup of sweet tea in that order." Jean raised her hand. "No arguments. Years ago you did this for me. Not the Brandy, but then I only had a fall at the church. Do you remember? I do because I was so very rude to you. The tea and the food helped. I feel for something a little more shocking than a fall though Brandy will be a welcome addition. Here you go." Jean said handing Jenna a glass with the Brandy in it. "Drink up."

Roy had taken over dishing up the food and making the tea.

Jenna felt the warmth of the Brandy as she drank it. Jean sat beside her, held her hand and said absolutely nothing which at that moment was the very right thing to do.

"Dinner is up." announced Roy.

"I think Jenna will be having another one of those after she has eaten as well. You are still quite pale."

"Thank you Jean but the tea should help."

"Let's not be hasty. There is nothing wrong with a Brandy or two. We may even join you. You may not feel like eating Jenna, but please have something."

Jenna who had been gazing at the food rather than partaking of it hadn't realised just how long she had been sitting at the table. Jean and Roy she noticed when she looked up after Jean's comment were over halfway through their meal."

"Thank you. Yes I will." she said and began eating slowly.

Jenna had just swallowed her last mouthful when the phone interrupted their very quiet dinner. Roy answered it and handed the phone to Jenna.

"Thank you so much for phoning. I have the Hazlett's with me. I am fine..... No need to tell the family just yet. Yes I will be here in the morning." Putting the phone down onto the table Jenna looked up and said to both Jean and Roy that was Sergeant Denton just checking up apparently he is coming by tomorrow to go over a few things.

"Jenna are you sure you don't want to come back to our place for the night?" Roy asked.

"Absolutely not. By the time I've had another Brandy which I am hoping is still on offer I will sleep like a baby."

KAREN PIVOTT

CHAPTER FOUR

Jenna quite unexpectedly had found herself to be the talk of the town.

Well in a small town to be fair someone involved in discovering a body was bound to be a topic of conversation immediately after the event had occurred. What was unexpected, was that a month had now passed and still the man had not been identified, and Jenna was still the talk of the town. Everybody knew a lot about what had happened, but in truth of course most people knew very little or nothing at all about the man Jenna had found dead.

Sergeant Denton had been visiting Jenna trying to jog her memory as they too were not getting any closer to the man's identity.

"As I was saying Mark we have a lot of new people coming into this small part of the town. Well it's not even part of the town is it? We are on the town boundary. A regular thoroughfare for thousands of people a week."

"That may be Jenna but the man has come from somewhere." The frustration in Mark's voice was obvious. Progress was needed but not forthcoming.

"Are you canvassing a wide enough area Mark?"

"The detective in charge certainly thinks so. Which brings me to why I have been sent to see you. I have been asked if you can come with me to the scene and talk to Detective Morris there."

"Very well, but I doubt I will have anything new to add. What time?"

"Two o'clock Wednesday afternoon."

"Why Wednesday?"

"Wednesday the weather conditions will be almost the same as the day you found the body."

"Oh I see" Jenna said "even the weather is factored in of course," and smiled as she said it. Mark smiled with her.

Wednesday came around all too quickly for Jenna, who met Detective Morris at the scene as arranged.

"As I've told you at the Station on earlier occasions it is not the obvious things that people recall."

"Yes I know. But as I have told you when I came upon the scene, what I told you is exactly what I saw, and the photographic evidence in your possession confirms that doesn't it?"

"Let's try this then. Where were you when you first noticed the man?"

"Right here."

"No. Where were you when you first noticed something untoward? Out of place? The general area?"

"Walk with me and I will show you exactly." Jenna said and began walking along the path coming to an abrupt halt.

"How do you know it was here exactly?"

"The grass here has been damaged. That is what drew my attention. I was quite cross because these grasses? Native grasses, have not long been planted, and it looked to me as though a scooter or skateboard had gone right through them causing the damage. I was thinking about all manner of things at the time as you do, and because I had stopped I was just beginning to get back to my walking speed when I noticed the object, and if you walk with me I will show you. Yes here. I first saw the object here, then when I got to here, yes by the pink paint on the curbing I realised the object was quite a bit larger than it had first appeared."

"Do you remember anything else?"

"A very sinking feeling in my stomach."

"No one else about?"

"A passing vehicle. White sedan. Nothing else."

"Thank you for coming."

"You know I have been thinking with the farming community and the new development we are getting a lot of people into our community. Imports if you will. Perhaps the man is not a New Zealander. Perhaps he has come from another country altogether. This is a small country and we have a little community as well."

"Someone must know him. Yes on that we do agree. Thank you again." He said as he dismissed Jenna who made her way back to her home.

The weather she thought on her return walk was similar, but the day was nothing like the day she had found the body, and still no one had claimed the man or reported him missing.

As Jenna unlocked her back door the phone began to ring. One of Jenna's phones was kept on the small shelf by the back door, she answered it, and listening as she continued to walk through to the kitchen saying, "Yes Jean. I will see you shortly then" then put the phone down. Filling the jug for a cup of coffee was attended to before promptly returning the phone to its waiting cradle by the back door. While there Jenna also put her shoes onto the shelf which was under the window. There were all sorts of little extras in this home. Each one had been put there for a specific purpose. The shelf by the back door was originally put there for the hand cleaner to sit on she had been told when she first viewed the house. The shelf under the window was for gumboots. The width of the vestibule off the back door was wider than normal so that when it was wet there was plenty of room to manoeuvre when taking wet coats off, and hanging them on the hooks on the wall on the right of the door. There was also a shelf above the hooks for hats to sit on. One of the legacies left in place was the old coffee mug holder which made a perfect cap holder. Jenna used that often.

I digress she admonished herself. Jean and Roy will be arriving with their house key. Very thoughtful of them. Even though Jenna now knew she could cope with the noise and the dust from the earthworks over the back, Jean and Roy had insisted on her having the option of staying at their place if things changed and she needed time out, and as if on cue Jenna heard their car arrive.

"Now remember" Roy said "You are welcome anytime day or night. Just make yourself at home."

"Thank you. I will pop around and check on things for you especially now the Leigh's are away to."

"Oh yes they are away in a couple of days." Jean said "Do keep in touch Jenna. You have our mobile number."

"You two go and enjoy your holiday. Catching up with old friends takes on a different meaning when you get up there in the numbers."

"Trust you I never gave that a thought." Roy said as they pulled away laughing.

Jenna watched them head off and removed a couple of dead heads from her Rose bush as she went back inside. The jug yes definitely time for a coffee she decided as she set about putting coffee granules into her mug, adding water, giving it a good stir and made her way to the armchair by the window. She put her cup onto the coaster Richard her grandson had made for her when he attended Intermediate school at the tender age of eleven. Jenna smiled as she remembered him bringing it to her, a look of absolute pride on his face.

"It's a bit wobbly in one place Nan but it should work all right." He had said. Jenna looked fondly at it reminding herself that it had worked very well for many years already and would be going strong for many years to come of that she was certain.

She put the foot rest out and sat back. Picked up her book from the small table, that also housed the coffee mug and coaster, and began to read.

With the coffee mug now empty and several pages more of the book read Jenna laid the book across her legs and looked out the window. Tomorrow she thought I will do some dead heading, and I will sweep along the edge of the driveway. The dust is building up there and the next time Jenna looked out of the window night had descended. Even with that revelation Jenna sat for some time until she was completely awake. The time on her wall clock told her it was well after eight o'clock.

"Perhaps a cup of Milo and a toasted sandwich." Jenna said as she rose from the chair. Still feeling tired she decided on the cup of Milo only and got ready for bed.

Jenna slept until the now familiar sound of earthmoving equipment sprang into life and roused her from a very deep sleep. Jenna got up and determined that today she would achieve more than she had yesterday, so straight after breakfast she began dead heading her roses. It was while she was doing this chore that she had a thought, put her secateurs' down and made a phone call. That phone call turned out to be the catalyst to identifying the man who Jenna had found dead.

Later that day Detective Morris arrived and brought Jenna the news.

"Well I don't know how to thank you, but thank you. What made you think of that?"

"Well I was tidying up the rose bush, when I remembered an article I had read just prior to leaving for Canada, about a new business in Hamilton where overseas workers between employment opportunities could go for additional work. It just popped out, and even though I felt you may have looked into that avenue already, I felt, well convicted you see. So I phoned you directly. So now we know the who, do we know the why?"

"One step at a time. We now have to notify people overseas of course. Find his family. News of this nature never improves with distance."

"Or with time." Jenna said.

KAREN PIVOTT

CHAPTER FIVE

It was well after the Christmas and New Year periods had passed before a picture began to emerge about the man Jenna had come across on her walk to the town boundary. His name was Stefan Molinsky. He was it turned out an orphan and was thirty three years of age. He had travelled across Europe to England, and found his way to Australia being employed as a ship hand before arriving on our shores by plane to work on a visitor's visa.

He had been in the South Island working with horticultural, and picking up other seasonal work on his way up the country. In the North Island he had picked up some work in the calving season on a dairy farm and when that had ended he began doing temporary work placements through the employment agency in Hamilton. He was by all accounts a good and reliable worker.

He had been working twenty minutes from Te Awamutu for only six weeks when he was murdered. The reason no one had reported him missing was simply a matter of the farmer and his wife being on their overseas holiday. There was one other worker who was also on the farm and he assumed the man had simply abandoned his job so he took steps to replace him with a local person who had returned to the district.

It transpired that Stefan had come across an altercation in the neighbouring town of Cambridge and had been stabbed then driven and dumped on the side of the road in the early hours of the morning.

Three men were charged with his murder, who had been tracked using CCTV.

"CCTV?" Jenna asked.

"Closed Circuit Television. There are signs up in and around the   shops."

"Yes the small camera things on the pole. So why did it take so long."

"We weren't looking in the right place for the right thing to start with. When we heard from the farmer that made all the difference. He wasn't too happy with his worker or the employment agency. In his view they should have been talking to each other when Stefan didn't turn up for work, but as you rightly pointed out we have a lot of new people living and working in our communities and many are transient so perhaps we need to take more care of them when they are with us?"

"Perhaps. Yes, but I am a bit confused as to how Cambridge came into the mix. What made you look there?"

"Sergeant Denton." Detective Morris said.

"He remembered an appeal the Police had done asking for people who witnessed an altercation to come forward around the same time and went over the CCTV information to see if our man was involved. The footage was not clear but when we pressed one of the men who had been identified in the altercation he admitted that the bystander had been hurt and dumped."

"Yes but how did it get pieced together?"

"Four men were seen leaving an alley way. One was moving much slower than the other three, and he was the one who laid a complaint with the Police. He said there were five men altogether one had tried to help him, but when the Police went to find him he had gone. What we didn't know was that the three men had a car and had gone back to get him."

"Heartless. I mean if they had gone to get him to take him to a hospital or called an ambulance that is one thing, but to pick him up like a piece of trash and dump him twenty or so minutes away and say nothing. It makes me feel ashamed to be a New Zealander."

"It's through your actions that we have found out who Stefan was. You have nothing to feel ashamed of. We have found a distant relative of his. A second cousin has come forward. Elena. She also was raised in an orphanage. Stefan had quite a bit of money. He had been sending it home so Elena is going to donate it to the orphanage where she works, to upgrade the babies' room. She is a lovely person and by all accounts so was Stefan. He was intending to work in Australia for a bit before returning to his homeland."

"All tidied up for you then. How long before the trial?"

"Well in this case there won't be a trial. The three men involved have pleaded guilty in both cases. Thank you for your help." Detective Morris said as he climbed into his car, and with a wave he was gone.

Jenna was watching the car pull away into the distance while thinking that at least Stefan had made a positive contribution to this world while he lived and as she looked up she saw a native wood pigeon the Kereru her favourite bird and a bird which was very rarely seen in this part of the town. A coincidence? No. Jenna said "thank you", and didn't care who heard her. Today was a good day and good days were to be embraced.

Jenna went inside and phoned Jean to bring her up to speed with all she had been told.

"I was wondering Jean if you would be free on Wednesday the week you return for lunch?"

"Not the Wednesday I'm afraid we have a hospital appointment at eleven. How about we get a Roast dinner from the Roast Hut and come to you for tea that night instead?"

"Pork, Lamb, Beef, Chicken anyone?" Roy called out.

"Lamb please and just a small one. I will do something for dessert. I hope all goes well." Jenna said without prying into why the hospital visit was necessary.

The day continued much as it had begun non-eventfully. Jenna was reading in her lounge by the window which got the afternoon sun and had dozed off to be awakened by the phone ringing.

"It's Jason. I only have a few minutes. I have rung mum. I passed the extra papers, and have been accepted for my papers for next semester. I am so thankful you were here to sort it out with me. I am still on track to have my degree even with the extra papers I had to do. Thank you."

"No need to thank me Jason you are the one who is doing the work. Will see you this Christmas?"

"I will let you both know. Bye for now. Bye" and with that he was gone.

Jenna couldn't have been more proud. She phoned Eden, Jason's Mum straight away.

"Jason has rung you then?"

"You must be very proud of him." Jenna said.

"I am. Not too proud of my behaviour though. I owe you an apology Jenna. I have been jealous of your relationship with Jason for some time, but you know that, and yet when I couldn't get to him and asked you to step in you didn't hesitate."

"Eden I think we need to acknowledge the positives we both bring to Jason's life. I have some resources that I am putting to good use there and you are his Mother. You will be there long after I have gone and what a fantastic son you have. He never ceases to amaze me. He's an achiever."

"All your children are achievers." Eden said.

"Yes they are. They achieve independently of me though. Their achievements were to impress their father in the first instance. Jason is achieving to make his life and yours better. That is the difference. No matter where Jason lives or works you will always be included in his life. He loves you a great deal, and he is loyal to a fault. I am quite envious really. You know Eden I thought I would be surrounded by my children and grandchildren and now I get to visit them once in a while. We talk often. We Skype as it is with you and Jason but you are family to Jason. Adam was family to our children, possibly because he wasn't around as much and then there were the revelations when he died. Even though they were adults themselves then, they felt a sense of freedom I think to continue on their own path. You are many years away from that."

"Thank you Jenna. How are the earth works progressing?"

"More progress every day and the building has started now. I hear and see a great deal of activity. I am enjoying the activity, people coming and going, and seeing the development coming together, but I will lose sight of it soon. They are building the fence in a week or so."

"Are you still happy there?"

"I am. Keep in touch and don't be a stranger you are always welcome here." Jenna said as she disconnected the call.

Jenna looked at the photo of Jason on her china cabinet and broke into a big smile.

The weeks flew by and before long Jenna was baking a dessert for her dinner guests. She had found some blackberries in her freezer so decided to make a good old fashioned blackberry and apple pie with a scoop of vanilla ice cream to go with it.

Jenna got down her crystal dessert bowls which normally sat at the rear of her cupboard. Passed down through the generations they were a one off design of a small run, which had sat on the shop shelf alone and when Jenna's great grandfather expressed an interest in them was offered them at a greatly reduced price. Given the year and the times that was in itself unprecedented. Given that her great grandfather was not a man of means and had gone into the shop to purchase a modest brooch puts the purchase into an even more incredible category. As the family story was told his fiancée of the day received the dessert bowls and fell in love with them. They were married and the dessert bowls, a cross between a side plate and a dessert bowl, had been used for special occasions since. The beauty of them still continues to be their design and functionality. They can be successfully used for an entrée, dessert, or small portion serve. Jenna was smiling as she placed them on the bench saying out loud "You are no use to me sitting in the back of the cupboard now are you?" not expecting to get a reply.

The pie was smelling delicious. The table was set and right on cue the sound of a car coming up the driveway prompted Jenna to move to the front door and open it for her guests.

Jenna opened the door with a large smile and open arms to welcome her guests in, but a man she had never seen before stood in her doorway.

CHAPTER SIX

"Mrs Mitchell?"

"Yes."

"Good afternoon, late afternoon as it happens. You don't know me I am working for the company who is developing the retirement village, just behind you. I wonder if I may come in and have a word with you."

"Do you have identification on you Mr?"

"I am so sorry. Bowen. Paul Bowen. Yes here is some validity for you." Mr. Bowen handed Jenna an official looking document addressed to him. An authorisation document she realised which had her name on it.

"Yes. Well I am expecting visitors any moment. Could you come back at another time?"

"Yes of course. It is just well. It will only take a few minutes I assure you."

"Like the door salesman only take a few minutes and half an hour later? I don't have half an hour you see."

"Just a couple of minutes."

"Yes very well you had better come in then. I see my name on that letter of authorisation you have there. What pray tell are people authorising you to do with me?"

"Not with you exactly more for you and us. The company would like a home close to the retirement village but not situated in it for the manager. We have looked at many of the properties here and would like to buy yours."

"Buy mine. I've not long lived here myself. I bought this property to see me out."

"We would make it worth your while."

"How many other property owners in this area have you spoken to?"

"One. We were considering two properties but of the two yours is the more viable."

"Why is that?"

"I can't go into that it is commercially sensitive."

"How very convenient for you Mr. Bowen it may be a figment of your imagination then this other property? No matter. As you are standing in my dining room I may as well ask, what is your offer? I don't mean to be rude, but as I said I am expecting visitors. Dinner guests as it happens."

"It smells as though they will be enjoying Blackberry and Apple pie? My nana used to make it. With a dollop of fresh whipped cream. Memories. Yes well in short the company would like to purchase your home as I've said. We wouldn't need to take possession until September."

"So you have already decided you are taking possession and we haven't discussed price or any other terms."

"Can I leave this letter with you? It spells everything out. All my contact details are there. Have a read and then give me a call? I am sure we can come to a mutually beneficial result for us both."

"Young man as I said, I have not long shifted here. I was in a beautiful old villa prior to coming here and I must say double glazing and insulation in a smaller space has does wonders. I can't tell you."

"Mrs. Mitchell I can assure you, you won't be any worse off. Just in a different location. All I am asking is that you consider it."

"Very well. I will let you know my decision in a few days. Is that agreeable to you?"

"Yes and thank you for your time. Beautiful plates. Quite unusual." He said as he moved passed the table on his way back to the front door.

As he was walking down the driveway Jenna's guests drove up to the front door.

Jean opened her door and stepped out of the car "Busy day I see Jenna."

"Yes. I have news to tell you and may need to get some advice from you. Change may be in the wind."

"Ditto."

Having enjoyed a lovely meal together the conversation began with the change that was happening to and for them and Jenna was saddened to learn it was not of a positive nature. Roy had once again to share his body with cancer and this time with the prognosis being terminal he was opting for quality of life not quantity.

Jean was surprisingly supportive of this. Jenna found it surprising because Jean was such a feisty, fighting sort of person.

"I must say Jenna I am surprised at how calm I am. I do believe though that Roy has made the right decision.   You are surprised as well I can tell. Now tell us what that man was doing here."

"I can show you. He left me a letter of authorisation with a view to purchase my property for the retirement village."

"Really? That is interesting." Roy said. "They approached Neville Chambers about this but his home is in a trust and the trustees would never go for it."

"Thank you Roy at least now I know that the other property does exist, and that our Mr Bowen is truthful.

Jenna took the letter which had been hand delivered to her by Paul Bowen to her lawyer Mr Benton.

"Well Jenna let me ask you, how do you feel about this?"

"To be honest I don't know. I wasn't thinking about selling, but then again I no longer have the rural view, and"

"You might consider it then?"

"There are other places in the town and on the town boundary that may come up. I don't have to rush after all."

"That is true but they will want a decision from you. Perhaps I could ask for an extension on that timeframe. It would give you some time to look around and see what your options are. Have you spoken to your family about this? They may want you to live with them."

"As lovely as that may sound too many people, for me. You know that my children live independently of me, and they are all overseas now."

"Jenna you don't have to sell."

"I know."

"What is it with you? Your last house was bought the same way. The person came to you."

"And that worked out well for everyone. I will give it more thought. Let me talk with Mr Bowen somehow I don't think a letter will be necessary."

"You are going to talk to your family about this Jenna?"

"Well that is not something I have decided to do just yet. I think I need to think on it some more."

"That is Jenna code for I will tell them when I have bought a place and have crossed the tees and dotted the eyes."

"Not this time. This time I really need to think about where to next if at all. I love my house. "

KAREN PIVOTT

CHAPTER SEVEN

Jenna had phoned Paul Bowen and had a discussion with him about her home becoming part of the Retirement Village package. Uncharacteristically she had brought the subject up with David who was adamant that she was under no obligation to sell, but pointed out that perhaps if she found something else equally valuable and viable there was nothing wrong with that either.

Jenna had put the phone down wishing that just for once someone else was there to make the decision and not her alone. This surprised Jenna because once she had begun making her own decisions she thought she would never again want or need to rely on someone else in the decision making process again. How things can change she mused.

Jean and Roy were very supportive of her right to decide and that of course was welcome but didn't actually help her to decide and Paul Bowen had extended the timeframe for her to make a decision so all in all Jenna felt as though her life was in limbo, or on hold in some way, and she felt this to be extremely uncomfortable.

On these occasions Jenna would take herself off for a walk somewhere. On this occasion she had decided upon walking around the Hamilton Gardens. It was during the week and there weren't a lot of people about so it was very restful. She walked and admired the gardens and sat to reflect. Before long two hours had passed and just as Jenna thought it was time to drive home, Jean and Roy were coming towards her.

"It is a lovely place to reflect isn't it?" Roy said as he sat beside Jenna.

"Yes it certainly is," Jenna agreed. Jean was sitting on the other side of Jenna when Roy said quietly and with conviction "We were called over here today to discuss a new treatment which is being trialled but I have decided Jenna it is going to be palliative care under Hospice for me." Jenna took hold of Jean's hand before asking "Are you sure Roy?" Roy smiled and said "Someone else may have better use of the opportunity than I." Then Jean added "Yes Jenna we are very sure."

Jenna squeezed Jean's hand and rose to leave. She affectionately rubbed Roy's shoulder as she stepped away from them.

The air was beginning to chill, summer was over and autumn was making its presence felt. Jenna got to her car and took a cardigan from the back seat and put it on. Her arms thanked her almost immediately and with her goose bumps beginning to recede she began the drive home. As she came into the town she saw a for sale sign being erected. Taking a mental note of the real estate company who was handling the listing Jenna decided to phone them as soon as she got home. Jenna phoned Paul Bowen to ask how long it would take for funds to transfer to her and got confirmation of the amount to be paid and the date the funds would be put into her account. Jenna's next phone call was to the Real Estate Agent to arrange a viewing.

Less than an hour later Jenna was viewing the home and it was almost too good to be true. A house younger than her current home, with everything you could want for and on the edge of a farm with the rural view Jenna had just lost, with the listing price less than the Retirement Village complex had offered her. Of the four entrance points to Te Awamutu this was the third Jenna had purchased on and she vowed the last. The house had been designed by a son for his mother whom he loved dearly, and it was that love that Jenna felt as soon as she entered the tree lined driveway.

There was such attention to detail plus the house was nestled on the section in such a way that the occupant felt secluded from the hustle and bustle of the traffic on their door step with the trees cleverly placed to absorb most of the traffic noise. Idyllic Jenna thought as she drove along the driveway to the house to meet the agent. Idyllic and comforting. What more could you want. She had walked through placing all her furniture in the house and before she got to the back door said "I am going to make an offer."

"Do you think you should get someone else to come through with you?"

"No thank you. I know the builder. I have spoken to him already about this house. Do I fill out the paperwork now for you or would you prefer to phone the owner directly first?"

"I could phone him now if you are sure?"

"I couldn't be more, sure. What are you waiting for?"

"It is just that I am... Well if you must know this is my first sale. On my own."

"Would you like me to phone the owner?"

"No. I will phone him now. He may be busy." Steve was saying as he dialled the number. "Mr. Carlton? Steve Davidson from, yes that Steve Davidson."

Jenna had continued her walk around the house and gardens and felt as if she had lived there for a very long time.

A short while later, Steve joined her in the garden with a big smile on his face. "He has accepted your offer. " The very words Jenna had known would be uttered.

As soon as Jenna got home she would phone the moving company then her lawyer Mr Benton.

None of this was a coincidence Jenna thought. Jenna would be relocated and unpacked before winter. "In four weeks" Jenna said thinking of the Kauri hat hanging on her wall. "You," "will be gracing a new view." Jenna smiled to herself at this comment because while she was viewing the house, just a short time ago, she had decided on the perfect wall to put the hat on. A wall that faced a large copper beech tree about the same age as the copper beech tree Jenna had often admired at a distance across the paddock at her neighbours when she lived in the large villa.

Remembering this reminded Jenna that she had some things to donate to the local Hospice Shop, sitting in her car so she dropped them off and made a mental note to self that there were a few other things that didn't need to be shifted to her new home, as well as her old pots and pans. Yes another trip to the Hospice shop would be made soon, and Jenna was sure that still more items could be added to the donation list, which would enable her to purchase new items which were currently on sale. With this thought in mind Jenna set off and after she had concluded her business she popped into see Jean and Roy.

"Jenna what a lovely surprise." Jean said as she opened the door.

"How is Roy today?" Jenna asked.

"Still making cups of tea for friends." Roy quipped as he came into view.

Jenna smiled and gave Jean's hand a squeeze. Roy had been losing ground for some time and was becoming quite frail, but his eyes had a sparkle to them still and his grin was just as cheeky as ever. He seemed even more relaxed now than he had at the Hamilton Gardens just a couple of hours ago.

"I see you have some activity in your street today." Jenna said as she walked through to the living room.

"Oh yes new neighbours. They are from Nigeria. He has a job in banking. They have two teenage boys. They introduced themselves to us a couple of days ago when they came to do the final inspection of the house."

"How are you Jean? You do know if you need a break I am more than happy."

"Yes Jenna of course but I feel our time now is so limited. Perhaps we could have a roast night again but here this time. Roy won't eat a large meal but he would enjoy the.."

"Normality of it." Jenna finished for her. "As would we all. Things have been rather curious this year on many fronts." Jenna said looking at Jean.

"Curious indeed." Roy said "You keep moving around the town literally. Itchy feet syndrome." Roy laughed.

With the conversation flowing it was easy to forget just how ill Roy had become, but then Roy had decided to carry on in spite of the cancer and for the limited time he and Jean did have, Roy was carrying on as normal just as he had set his mind to do, all be it a bit more slowly, and with considerably less vigour than Jenna had seen him exhibit before.

CHAPTER EIGHT

The four weeks flew by and Jenna was in the process of cleaning her now empty house when there was a knock on her door.

Jenna got up and opened the door to Paul Bowen. "Mr. Bowen, I wasn't expecting to see you! I thought we had concluded our business."

"We have I just thought I would pop in to see you are okay with everything. It all happened very quickly and I was passing when I saw your car on the driveway."

"Yes I am fine. I am cleaning the house as you can see. You really do arrive at the most inconvenient times. Is it a knack you have for everyone or just me?"

"Maybe it is that you are busy when I call in, or that I call in unannounced, and it is Paul."

"Well Paul as this is likely to be the last time I will see you, I thank you for calling in. Very thoughtful. You know even though it has all come about quickly as you say it has worked out well."

"And you are completely shifted into your new place?"

"Yes. The movers did everything, and apart from having to hunt out the odd thing I am thank you. I still have a couple of small things to do. I am going to replicate a couple of the things I have found very practical here, but apart from that I am all done," and with that Paul smiled shook her hand and left.

Mental note to self, purchase shelving unit for gumboots to stand on at the back door vestibule, and get a coat stand for the garage, call in and see Jean and Roy on the way home. Get flowers for Jean.

As can happen time got away on Jenna but to her credit she managed to get everything done. Jean loved the flowers and was grateful for the impromptu visit. Roy was sleeping but that wasn't a surprise these days. Jenna stayed for a cup of coffee and invited Roy and Jean for a visit.

"What time of the day would suit Roy best?"

"How refreshing." Jean said. "Someone who openly considers Roy. Do you know we were at the Supermarket just yesterday and a person we both know came up to us and spoke about Roy as if he wasn't even there with us present? I have to tell you Jenna infuriating."

"You do know Jean some people just don't know how to communicate in a situation that they don't have experience of themselves. Just saying."

"Making excuses for them more like. You always see the good in people Jenna even when the bad is blatantly obvious or on display."

"Would Roy cope with lunch?"

"Yes. Lunch would be lovely. Would Wednesday suit you?"

"Any day of the week suits me where you two are concerned. See you Wednesday then and Roy can have a sleep in one of the spare rooms if he needs to."

"Thank you." Jean said as Jenna walked through the door to go to her car, absolutely oblivious to the pertinent statement Jenna had made. The mind is a selective beast, had Jean thought about it she would have realised that she herself had not communicated well to, or about the situation Jenna had found herself in when at Adam's funeral the second family appeared.

Wednesday came around all too quickly. Jenna had lunch organised and had an effect began setting the table when the phone rang, "Hello Jenna speaking".

"Jenna it is Jean. I am in a bit of a bind. Roy is not good today Jenna. He is insistent that he comes for lunch. Honestly Jenna he does not look at all well."

"Well Jean, it just so happens that I was getting lunch ready, how about I just put it into the chilly bin and bring it to you instead?"

"I think if it is not too much trouble it would be an absolutely perfect solution for everyone. See you soon then Jenna." Jenna immediately began returning the plates, cutlery, glasses, and serviettes to the respective homes in the kitchen. The table now cleared Jenna began to take the food from the bench that was covered, carefully placing it in the Chili-bin. And less than twenty minutes later Jenna and Jean had not only set the table, and dished the food up, but had taken a plate of food through to Roy to enjoy at his leisure. Jane and Jenna found themselves sitting together and talking more than they were eating. This concerned Jenna as often these days Jean did not seem to be eating very much at all. As the conversation progressed Jenna managed to bring the subject up in a very diplomatic way. "Jean you are eating enough yourself these days aren't you?"

"I have to admit, and this is just between ourselves you understand, well there are days, when I really do not feel like eating at all. On those days I tend to snack, healthy things, fruit, nuts, and the occasional piece of chocolate. I still cook every day of course, but it does seem a waste of food and time when the two recipients seem to struggle with the thought of even eating."

"Jean if there is anything, and I mean anything that I can do to help, let me do it."

"Thank you Jenna, but you have done so much already and it has been months. You know they said he had advanced cancer and the timeframe was short. That's what they said and it has been nearly, well nearly," Jean's words were interrupted by an eruption of sobbing and tears flowing down her cheeks from have spilled over from her eyelids. Jenna reached over to her and taking her hand said quietly, "I would say a few months over one's entire lifetime is quite short. Now let's not get hung up on timeframes. One day at a time, and just so you know, I am not counting the days, at all I am here to help you both. Let me go and get the tray from Roy, and then I will make us all a nice cup of tea."

With that Jenna let Jean's hand go and went in to see Roy, who was sitting up in bed with an empty plate.

"That was delicious Jenna. You know I haven't felt like eating for a few days but just knowing that jean was to have company even though I'm losing ground made all the difference. It is harder on her you know. It is times like these I wish we had been blessed with a family of our own."

"Now Roy there is no point is there of thinking like that. You and Jean are the family. It has taken me a long time to work that out. There was Adam and I, then along came the children, then the children left and I thought there was Adam and I, but as we all now know, there was also Adam and "

Roy's words interrupted Jenna "Yes, we now do know that one family wasn't enough for Adam and look where that took everyone. Oh Jenna here I am going on and expecting you to help us through and you are very much still in the grieving process yourself."

"Well I don't think about it like that. I am just getting on. You do don't you. I have been so busy."

"You must have days Jenna. Surely? You were with Adam, married to Adam for a long time."

"I think it was the shock of finding out I didn't really know Adam to be the person I thought he was. I feel it is my fault, that I was lacking him in some way. There are days when I just want of ask him for forgiveness and there are other days when I just want to….. Let's just agree that there are days when, I think uncharitable thoughts when it comes to Adam!"

"Oh Jenna most people would be yelling from the rooftops what a total disappointment the man was. Jean has always said you see only the good in people even her and all know that Jean can be acerbic."

"Well right now all you need to know Roy is that Jean, your Jean is being nothing other than loving and totally devoted to you and I might say that is taking tremendous courage. I admire her. You Roy Hazlett lucked in there."

"And don't I know it. Thank you Jenna. Would it be too much to ask if perhaps these Chilli-Bin meals happened on a more regular basis?"

"Not at all shall we say every Wednesday and Saturday for the time being?"

"Saturday is a weekend day Jenna."

"Weekdays, weekend days, makes no difference to me. These days I am able to choose what I do without interruption seven days a week a true luxury I can tell you." With Roy's eyes growing heavy Jenna picked up his plate and left him to drift back to sleep. On her return to the dining room she saw that the dining table had been cleared and Jean had made a pot of tea. Jenna put the tray on the kitchen bench and rinsed the empty plates and cutlery before loading them into the dishwasher.

"Jenna." Jean said. "Not another word" Jenna interrupted her "Roy and I have decided that Chilli-Bin meals are on twice a week from now on, and I am afraid Jean you will have the inconvenience of putting up with me every lunch time each Wednesday and Saturday for quite some time. Now let's have that tea shall we?"

"If you are coming twice a week you may need something a little stronger than tea." Jean said as she looked at Jenna with love and appreciation in her eyes.

KAREN PIVOTT

CHAPTER NINE

A month on and the Chill-Bin meals were something that both Jenna and the Hazlett's looked forward to. Jenna realised a new routine had emerged quite naturally in her new home. Jenna also acknowledged that although comfortable Roy was becoming weaker with each visit. He still had good days, but as he had defied the timetable already it was only a matter of time, and the toll was showing on Jean.

Jenna had started staying later on a Wednesday and Saturday so Jean could get shopping done or just have a break from the house after their lunchtime meal.

Jenna had started writing again as well. Every morning she would spend two hours at least letting her mind wander while her fingers did the walking across her keyboard. Characteristically Jenna had never been an early riser but of late she found herself waking at five o'clock in the mornings and not being able to get back to sleep decided to get up make herself a cup of tea and write for a bit. Jenna was keeping this information to herself for the moment. She didn't want her family to know she was working on less sleep. They asked her all sorts of questions on the regular Skype calls now.

"You know David one would think you were there directing things while I gave birth to you. I have been managing on my own for a while now. If anything is amiss I will tell you and your siblings." Was one of the comments made at one of the more recent Skype calls Jenna recalled one very sunny morning as she had concluded her writing session for the morning. On that particular occasion two hours had become four, and being a Wednesday it was a very good thing that Jenna had set the Chilli-Bin lunch engagement into her computers calendar. Set with a reminder no less. Jenna began getting their lunch organised when the phone rang.

"Hello. Jenna speaking." She said with a smile on her face as she answered the phone.

"Yes good morning Jenna." Jenna recognised the crisp no nonsense voice on the phone that needed no introduction and smiled as the introduction followed anyway, "It is Judy your publisher, or should I say the publisher you dumped."

"I hardly think retiring is in the same league as dumping Judy and a very good morning to you. How are you?"

"I was sitting having my morning coffee and thinking how I might goad you out of retirement with just one or maybe two more books. The truth is I miss working with you. You are the easiest in my stable of writers Jenna. A breath of fresh air."

"A fairly old breath I would say. What is going on Judy? Are some of your filly's giving you cause for concern?"

"The truth is, no one is writing what you write."

"You mean no one is writing the fluff I believe you called it which allowed my retirement to commence in the first place. The fluff that young people can live without. The fluff Judy that is, correct me if I am wrong, 'outdated and no longer fits in the modern world' they were your words just a few years ago were they not?"

"Yes they were, and let's not pretend that you were forced into retirement. You are the one who mentioned the 'R' word first."

"As it happens Judy I am working on something and before you say let me see it, let me just say I am not sure if it is something you would publish at all. It is not a fluff piece."

"If it is not fluff why are you writing it?"

"In short to help people." Jenna replied. "Now I am sorry Judy but I have a lunch engagement to get ready for."

"Will you send me an outline or maybe just a couple of lines about the book to have a look at?"

"Maybe in a day or two. Let me think on it."

"Excellent. If you are wanting to help people I can help you reach many people."

"I will email you Judy." Jenna said with a crispness of her own and hung up the phone.

As soon as Jenna got the food into the Chilli-Bin she paused and looked at the green pasture out of her kitchen window and silently told herself off. Jenna Mitchell what were you thinking talking to Judy like that, while at the same time Judy was talking to Tania one of her editors saying "I was quite surprised at the tone Jenna took with me. Not just the words, the tone. So unlike her."   Tania smiled and quietly said "About time."

"Pardon?"

Tania replied "Just give her some time. There could well be a lot going on with Mrs Mitchell. Did you ask her how she was?"

The look Tania received answered that question, "I will just leave this with you then?" Tania said placing a manuscript on the desk for Judy to look at and taking her leave.

Tania had a smile on her face for the rest of the day. Of all the writers she had worked with Mrs Mitchell was the most polite, the most accommodating and the most tolerant of Judy's temperament something must be happening in her world Tania thought to speak harshly to Judy and not before time Tania also thought. Judy would have to do some work there. Mrs. Mitchell for all her niceness wasn't a push over by any means. Tania recalled a conversation they had had years before when Tania had just started working there. "Mrs. Mitchell can't you add some action or something?" She'd asked.

"Tania I don't have to add action. My readers are living action packed lives every day. They read my books because I give them an escape from all that."

"Yes but how much action can a stay at home mum have in their day?"

"In their working day? When you are a stay at home mum, if you get that opportunity we will have this conversation then. Until then is there anything else?"

"No. No its fine. Look I just thought."

"Tania I am hoping we have a long, healthy and happy working relationship let's not trip ourselves up on the journey. I write what I write and Judy publishes it. That is the way of it. Now let me ask you a question. Do you want to change what Judy wants me to write? And with that Jenna smiled and winked at Tania.

"I hadn't thought of it quite like that." Tania replied.

"Exactly. By any and all means we must deliver what the reader expects. That is the Judy motto is it not?"

"Yes Mrs. Mitchell it is. Thank you for reminding me. Rather you than Judy."

"It is Jenna. Maybe down the track I could write something different? But not at the moment."

"You will never be Jenna to me. You are Mrs. Mitchell because I have learned so much from you already. I just get". Jenna finished her sentence for her.

"Frustrated. Tania you are very good at what you do. I have worked with a few editors over the years so I know a good editor when I am working with one. When the day comes I will work with you and only you, on the something different. Deal?"

Yes Jenna thought I will add into the email that Tania is to be my editor on this book. I wonder what Tania is doing these days? Jenna thought as she loaded the Chilli-Bin into the car.

As she pulled up to a waiting Jean, Jenna saw an excitement in her friend's eyes that she had missed.

"I can see something is up. Spill the beans."

Jean took the Chill-Bin out of the boot and put it in the kitchen. "Jenna Roy and I were wondering if you would write a book for people on how to live while the life of their loved one is coming to an end. There are lots of books out there written by people who are battling cancer or living with disease or disabilities, but there doesn't seem to be much written for the people who are caring for those who are dying. People say we are living longer, but I look at Roy and it is a case of he is dying longer."

Jenna smiled. "Well actually Jean I was going to talk to you about just that. How would you feel if I used some of your experience in the book?"

"If it is going to help others deal with the roller coaster I am more than happy and so is Roy. You know he said to me just this morning if we had known it was going to take this long, we could've set things up a bit differently."

"Well let's do a chapter on that then. The Plan B chapter. How does that sound."

"You've already started writing haven't you?"

"Writing is a release for me. I called it my anti-depressant when the kids were younger."

"Yes I remember that time well myself. Treat the housewife not the issue. One would hope we have moved on from that."

"One would hope. But have we? I will just pop in and see Roy and let him know his lunch has arrived."

CHAPTER TEN

The weeks continued to roll by and
the season changed yet again. Winter was
always a bleak time. Many clouded days
with the interruption of rain and wind
quite common. The temperatures went
from cool, to cold, to what some might say
freezing, and the odd day of sunshine
shone through the all the senses
reminding us of summer coming again.

Jenna had heard from Judy her
emails like her conversations were crisp
and to the point. 'Sorry Jenna Tania is
unavailable. She is a home maker now.
Can you believe it?' Of course Jenna
could believe it. Tania was now in her mid

to late thirties and was no doubt relishing her time as a home maker. That noble yet unsung profession for way too long and still it would seem undervalued by some.

Now Jenna thought what was her partner's name? Bas? Sebastian. Sebastian Clarke. Jenna looked up the on line phone directory and noted down three numbers. Lucky call number two found Tania.

"Mrs. Mitchell how on earth did you find me? I know Judy would not have passed my information on to you or anyone. She was not happy when I left. Not happy at all."

"I remembered your partner's name and hoped you were still together. Actually thinking about that now that was presumptuous. What if you had left him and was with someone else?"

"Believe me he would not hold back in informing you of that, if that was the case. What can I do for you?"

"I was hoping you would edit my 'something different' book."

"Thank you but apart from the fact that Judy would never employ me again I am way too busy with the children these days."

"So you have discovered your own action packed life now, is that what you are telling me?"

"Funny you should bring that up. I read one of your earlier books and I now understand why they were so, or should I say are so popular. I think you may have found a whole new audience these days."

"Really? I am pleased you like them. I think I can talk Judy around even if it is for only this one book. If not there is the electronic platform for Indie authors these days so that is an option. No pressure. I remember the parenting days well."

"What is this something different book about?"

"Dying longer. A non-fiction book."

"Let me talk to Bas. What is your number there?"

And with that Jenna knew that she would very shortly be phoning Judy to pave the way for Tania to edit her book. With only a few of the chapters done Jenna realised she would need to get more written, and with that thought she set about working on the next chapter.

The book was taking shape. The emphasis was different now to what Jenna had begun with requiring the first few chapters to be rewritten, but Jenna was not unhappy with that. Jean and Roy did bring an authoritative tone and realistic view point to Doctor's visits, Hospice nurse visitation and the isolation of their situation, which Jenna found was common place amongst other people dealing with the same or similar situations. Jenna felt blessed that she had been spared this scenario with Adam's death.

The weeks were slowly passing and the book was coming along nicely. Tania had read the first few chapters and she was pleasantly surprised, which surprised her. The book far from being sombre and morbid was practical with light hearted moments peppered through it quite skilfully. The biggest surprise of all for Tania was the flexibility with which Judy allowed her to edit the book. The fact Tania was a good editor was not in doubt, the feeling of enjoying editing after a break when all her energy, enthusiasm and commitment was now firmly on raising their family that was a revelation to Tania.

"You know Tania the advent of technology has made all our lives different and some parts of them much better."

Tania recalled Jenna mentioning one day when they were talking about line 27 page 12 chapter two. What a funny detail to recall Tania thought as she hung out the washing.

In the neighbouring rural township Jenna was having a chat with Roy as she cleared his lunch tray away, while Jean rinsed their dishes in the kitchen.

"You know Jenna I am trying to get Jean to look at smaller places. Maybe a townhouse or a unit? This place has stairs and is so big. The ceilings are high and I am concerned."

"I can see you are, but Roy all your memories are here. The memories the two of you have built together over the years, and perhaps Jean just isn't ready to let them go quite yet."

"Memories are in your head Jenna you take them with you wherever you go."

"Yes I agree with that, but for a time it is nice to be surrounded by the feel of them as well. This Roy is something I know a little about. You know when we decided to shift to our dream house and we were packing things up it was a slow process and then Adam passed unexpectedly. When I did the actual shift and was going through the boxes of things they seemed out of place somehow. I do wonder if that is why I felt so unsettled in the Villa. You know when Mason knocked on the front door and offered to buy the house I realised it was a relief. I loved the house but I was being freed from it almost. Well not quite that."

"Being let out of a contractual arrangement that wasn't working for you? Yes I get that."

"You do know of course that I am the wrong person to talk to about downsizing. I do live in a four bedroom home with two living spaces and a separate dining space, with a separate laundry two toilets a bathroom and an ensuite."

"And you love it."

"Yes I do."

"I understand that Jenna and then you do have your family on occasion."

"Well I haven't yet but there is always that possibility. The truth of it is I like room. I like having my writing room. I can go in there, into my own little world and create, keep busy, enjoy the view from the large window, pastures in winter with a floral border in the spring. It is so peaceful. Very self-indulgent. "

"What are you two talking about in there?" Jean called out "You are holding up the dishes."

"That's a picture I never thought I would have to think about." Roy said with a grin "Holding dishes up."

Jenna laughed with him and headed for the kitchen where Jean was waiting. Yes light hearted moments were rare but very welcome.

"He was bending your arm about the townhouse wasn't he?"

"We were exchanging points of view."

"I won't do it." Jean said with a tone of defiance.

"Of course you will. You will find the right place for you when you are ready which is not quite yet. The good news is I have amassed lots of experience in the packing department."

Rubbish. The movers shifted you across town this last time. They did everything."

"Exactly. As I said I have lots of experience in the packing department and that by far was the best shift I have ever done." With that comment Jean found herself first cracking a small smile and then laughing, with Jenna.

On her return home Jenna added the dilemma of those soon to be left behind face when their loved one puts forward ideas they see as a benefit for them. Another layer of expectation added to the heap perhaps? Preparing for the loss without them being there to endure the loss is all part of the process Jenna reasoned. The loved one left behind of course is mostly focussed on their loved one still here and doing all they can to make them feel at ease, loved, comforted. What a conundrum it all is Jenna thought. It all gets quite messy. That being said nothing prepared her for the tearful start to the Saturday luncheon that week.

On her arrival she was met at the door by Jean who had obviously been crying and as she went to extract the Chill-Bin from Jenna burst into a flood or unadulterated tears.

"Jean whatever is the matter?"

"You need to ask Jenna? He's dying." Jean said.

Jenna was momentarily taken aback. Of course Roy was dying that was a given and had been for many months so

Jenna was somewhat confused by the outburst.

"He wants a plain pine coffin. Plain. How's that going to look? I am going to be seen as the miser of the town. Wouldn't even send him off in a decent coffin and it is not the cost. I mean we can afford a nice looking coffin."

"What has brought all this on Jean?" Jenna asked as the Chilli-Bin was put down in the kitchen.

A voice from the neighbouring room piped in "We've had the funeral director here today Jenna. He has been orchestrating his next retirement home." Roy said.

"Really Roy!" Jean said with a tone of exasperation present.

"Nice to see you up Roy."

"Yes well I thought I let him know he would have to wait a bit yet before I check out, and he, cheques in." Roy said chuckling.

"He has been like this all morning." Jean said. "I am at my wits end."

"What is the issue Roy?" Jenna asked.

"Well it's not the price although that is, well you know don't you Jenna."

"Unfortunately I do. Why do you want a plain pine coffin?"

"My father worked in a timber mill back in the day and he always said the closer you work with nature the better. Good for the earth. Since then I have only ever wanted a plain pine box. Jean has always known that. Then this fellow arrives with the cushioning and the multiple timber options and I don't see myself going out like that."

"One concession he does agree to handles. One step up from rope." Jean said with a sarcastic tone that only revealed itself when she was under stress or not in a good place at all.

"What is it about the coffin that upsets you so much Jean?"

"Well I guess if I am honest I saw myself dying first so I never really thought about it overly much until today. There were the brochures and the..."

"Well practiced sales pitch." Roy added.

"Jean there is a lady in town who runs a coffin club for people who want to purchase their own coffin and decorate it. How about I give her a call and get her to come and speak with you both?"

"How low can people get. Making money off the dead." Roy said.

"I think you might be surprised by what she has to say." Jenna said as she took out her phone.

"Yes hello Pamela. Jenna Mitchell speaking. Yes the very same. Pamela I have a couple of friends who are deciding on Coffin options and I wondered would you mind paying them a visit. If it's no trouble. Yes two o'clock will be fine. I will text you the address. Thank you so much. Well that was meant to be I would say. Two o'clock today. No harm in listening to what she has to say now is there."

"I may be sleeping by then." Roy said.

"Somehow I doubt that." Jenna said giving him a knowing look.

"I will dish up lunch then." Jean said, and lunch turned out to be a very quiet one indeed.

All the lunch dishes had been cleared, washed and put away by the time Pamela arrived.

Jenna introduced Pamela to the Hazlett's. "Roy, Jean I would like you to meet Pamela Tiggs. Now Pam can you explain your coffin club to these two."

"Gladly, but really Jenna you could do it just as well."

"How's that?" Roy asked.

"You haven't told them have you? Jenna funded our pilot programme."

"Pam."

"Yes well we help people prepare for death either their own or their loved ones. We provide the plain coffin and people decorate it however they like. Many people use their coffins as coffee tables or book shelves until they go in them. Some people just store them in the garage. The cost is minimal and the family or loved ones get to have an input."

"What kind of input?" Jean asked.

"The colour of the coffin. A painting on the inside of the lid perhaps. The fabric they want to lie on or not. Many people just want to be wrapped in a favourite cotton sheet and placed into their box like that. It is up to the individual."

"I see." Jean said.

"I have a pamphlet with my details for you. Have a read. Talk about it and give me a call."

"I wouldn't be able to participate in the project." Roy said.

"You might be surprised. If you know what you want, I am sure I can find volunteers that will be more than happy to help you have exactly that."

"What's the cost?" Roy asked.

"The coffin. Time. Imagination and love." Pamela said and with that took her leave.

"Jenna why have you never mentioned this to us?" Jean probed.

"Not exactly dinner conversation is it? And to be perfectly honest I thought you would have had all this sorted. You have pretty much sorted everything else. Let's be frank shall we. Coffins. Death. They are a private matter."

"What made you start this project?" Jean asked.

"The cost of Adam's funeral. I got to thinking about all the families, people who do not have the means for an expensive funeral, and I can tell you that funerals are expensive even at the lower end. People are so vulnerable on the day. A man with a lovely suit arrived, and he had his folder and there were no prices on display. I just got overwhelmed with the choices and everything. David arrived and said he would take care of it, which he did, but even so. I still see the silver handles on the casket, and Adam well he preferred gold. Your mind does funny things when you are grieving. I just thought perhaps there was a better way, and I read about a coffin club in an article on the internet. I got talking to Pam about it one day when she was buying books from the shop, and we had a few follow up conversations about it. She thought it was a great idea so I let her run with it."

"Can I have my plain box?"

"Roy you can have whatever you like." Jenna said "That's the beauty of it."

"I bet the funeral directors don't like it?" Roy said.

"Actually we have found them to be most accommodating."

"Tiggs." Roy said "Why do I know that name?"

"Could we at least have a picture on the lid?" Jean asked.

"If I am having my plain pine box I could allow you to put a picture on the lid if that will stop the tears. Jean could you help me to bed?" Roy asked his eyes becoming heavy.

"Why don't I help as well?" Jenna offered looking over at Jean.

"A ménage a trois. All my dreams have come true. Better late than never." Roy said in speech that was becoming somewhat slurred.

By the following Wednesday Jean had a picture Roy had agreed to sorted out for his coffin with the cheeky quip 'Roy's final resting place. Good for the earth, good on him.' Underneath it. They had even agreed on the wreath.

Jean was going to meet the group on their meeting day the next Thursday. She had measured Roy for the right coffin size, paid for the coffin, and spoken to the funeral director who was very understanding.

"I do believe there is more to this coffin club project than you are telling us." Jean said over that Wednesday lunch.

"Good came out of a bad situation shall we just leave it at that." Jenna answered.

"So not just about Adam then?"

"Jean there are times in one's life when things happen and later other things happen and circumstances allow one to help. I love helping. What is the point of having, when you are not able to give, when you are a person who gets the warm fuzzies when you give? Many years ago I learned that sometimes money is not what is important. Money helps, but money doesn't always solve the issue. I was able to help and for many people their issues around death have been eased, healed, handled. I was in the right place, with the right person, at the right time. I am taking the win. You will win as well."

"I looked up the Tiggs name and found there had been a loss of a husband and two children in a car accident and their mother Pamela was hospitalised for quite some time. She had told the paper the worst part was not being able to put her family to rest."

"As I said. Right place, with the right person at the right time." Jenna reiterated.

"Do you want to come with me Jenna?"

"No you will be fine. I think you need to do this on your own Jean to be honest. They are a lovely group."

"Healing one death at a time?" Jean asked.

"Maybe but everyone is there for their own reasons."

CHAPTER ELEVEN

Another month had passed and the book was now with Judy in the process of being published. Roy and Jean had read over the draft before it was given to Judy. Tania's input as always had been invaluable and as for Jenna she felt it was a very good practical piece of writing and wondered why she had never written non-fiction before now.

With Christmas rapidly approaching Jenna was being put under pressure on many fronts. The families in Australia wanted her to spend Christmas with them, but due to their work commitments that meant Jenna would be travelling again. Which under normal circumstances would have worked well but this Christmas Karla and Bryce were in Darwin, while David, Deanna, Richard and Stephanie were in Melbourne. Then there was Vincent and Brittany to consider in Canada who had come out the Christmas before with her parents who wanted Jenna with them as well. Not to mention Jason and Eden who had decided to spend Christmas together in the States and had invited Jenna to join them as well. Too many choices and Jenna although she hadn't voiced it to anyone was quite tired. Since her arrival home earlier in the year things had been quite busy.

It was a very busy Monday when Jenna arrived home to the phone call that put all thoughts of Christmas well to one side.

"Jenna I have had to admit Roy to Hospice this afternoon."

"I will be right there Jean." Jenna said as she put her perishables in the fridge and her frozen goods in the freezer.

On her arrival at the Hospice Jenna found Jean sad and relieved almost simultaneously.

"He asked me to phone them." Jean explained. "He said. 'If you are going to stay on at the house I am not going to die in it.' Jenna I feel so selfish. "

"In all the time I have known you both, Roy has always done the right thing for him and by you." Jenna said as she put her arms around Jean. "We'd best go in." Jean said.

Together they sat by Roy's beside talking quietly, and having quiet moments to remember their times together and separately. Jenna and Jean went to have a cup of tea at seven thirty and when they arrived back at Roy's room he had passed away.

The funeral was a very quiet affair. The church community were there. There was talk about the coffin of course but not of a negative nature. Jenna stayed until after the wake and offered to stay the night with Jean but she declined.

"I will be all right Jenna. Thank you though. Perhaps you could pop in tomorrow morning if you're not too busy?"

And so for a time a new routine was in place, and slowly all the plans discussed by Roy and Jean for this eventuality were implemented.

For Jenna this meant more free time and during one of these days Jenna decided she would spend Christmas at home alone this year. This was important to Jenna. It was another part of closure for her. Jenna had kept herself so busy since Adam's death. Christmas alone without family, friends or Adam. It seemed to be the right time.

At their regular Saturday lunch Jean told Jenna that she was going to spend time with the friends she and Roy had spent time with earlier in the year. Tagged onto the end of that piece of news Jean asked Jenna to accompany her, on her return in the New Year when she started to look for a new place.

"I know I said I was going to stay put, but I can see now that all Roy's points were valid. I need somewhere that is more manageable."

"There is no need to rush into it. By all means look at what is available.   I always find that when the time is right the house actually finds you."

"Is that really your experience Jenna?"

"It seems to have been the last few times."

"You are happy where you are now aren't you? I mean you have settled in?"

"Yes. If I am honest I have settled in rather quickly, and yes I feel completely at home now."

"And the hat?"

"If only hats could talk Jean my hat would have quite the story to tell." Jenna said with a smile remembering that just the morning before she had shifted the hat onto the opposing wall where the morning sun caught its edges nicely giving it quite a golden glow.

Jenna on her arrival home started Skyping the family to tell them of her decision to spend this Christmas at home on her own. She would contact them all of course and they would chat.

Stephanie was the most vocal about it but even she conceded that perhaps a bit of time to catch-up with yourself wouldn't hurt.

Jenna thought this was an interesting phrase especially as Jenna hadn't got behind herself in the first place. Once those calls were made Jenna felt at peace and with Jason's call the only one left to make she made herself a cup of tea before Skyping him.

"Hello. You just caught me between events."

"I thought your school day had ended. Shall I call back?"

"No. You're not coming for Christmas are you?"

"No Jason. I am staying at home."

"You will be alone."

"No I will be at home on my own."

"You are looking tired. Are you getting enough sleep?"

"Yes but I can always do with a bit more. Have a great Christmas. I have put something small in the post for you and your mum you should have it well before Christmas. No opening."

"Until Christmas day. Yes I remember."

"I won't hold you up. Bye." And with that Jenna had terminated the call, when the phone began ringing. Jenna made her way to where she had last put the phone down and answered it.

"Jenna its Jean I have got myself in a bit of a predicament. Can you come?"

"Of course Jean I will be right there," and before she gave it any thought at all Jenna was picking up car keys and driving to Jean's aid.

On her arrival, Jean surveyed the scene and assessed the situation swiftly ascertaining an ambulance was needed.

"I blame myself Jean. I should have asked you what your predicament was."

"I should have rung the ambulance myself but I couldn't get to the phone and by the time I reached it I was fairly tuckered out. How bad is it? My leg feels a little sticky."

"I doubt you will be running a marathon anytime soon." Jenna answered.

"So there is a silver lining then?" Jean said.

Jenna looked over the scene and having found a pen and some paper sketched it out and wrote down Jean's recollections before she found herself in a heap on the floor.

"I was trying to get the bottled beetroot down to go with my dinner tomorrow night. I felt the step ladder wobble and to be honest I can't remember much else until I thought I needed to ring for help and then I couldn't see the phone."

"And what time was this? What time Jean did you climb up to get the Beetroot?"

"Just after two o'clock."

"I see" said Jenna looking at her watch which was showing the time to be a quarter past five meaning Jean had been on the floor for nearly three hours."

The sound of the ambulance siren brought some sense of order to the chaotic scene around her. The ambulance officers took details from Jean and Jenna while making their observations. Jean was put onto a stretcher then loaded into the ambulance. Jenna found a small bag and put a night gown, underwear and toiletries in the bag. Picked up the step ladder and returned it to its normal home. Tidied up the floor area where Jean had landed taking some of the spices along with other items off the shelf as she descended, and gave a prayer of thanks that it was just a compound fracture by the looks of things. X-Rays would reveal if there was anything else.

Looking up at the cupboard door still wide open Jenna decided it could stay that way until a taller more agile person was available to help empty those cupboards out completely.

"Why the beetroot?" Jenna said out loud and then she remembered. Tomorrow would have been Roy's birthday and Jean always served beetroot with salad on Roy's birthday. It was Jean's homemade beetroot that sealed the picnic and the union for life for Roy. Jenna remembered there was talk about the beetroot many years after they had wed.

Jenna locked the house and made her way to the hospital. Jean was being prepared for surgery. Along with the compound fracture there were two more fractures in her leg and she had also broken her shoulder.

Jenna left her things and advised the nurse on duty that she would be back the following day to see Jean asking her to let Jean know.

On her way home Jenna stopped on the side of the road looking at the pastures spread before her feeling very blessed, and praying for a speedy recovery for Jean.

Jenna stopped at the roast hut for a small dinner which she took home and ate with great enthusiasm. She was actually very hungry she realised. After she had finished she phoned the Minister and the Prayer Chain leader and let the church grapevine do its thing. Jenna knew by the following mid-day people would have been contacted to visit Jean while she was in the hospital so that every day she would have a fresh face to see.

Even when you are on your own there is no need to be alone. Jenna thought as she laid her head down on her pillow with heavy eyelids. She slept soundly until quite late the next morning.

CHAPTER TWELVE

Jean had been in hospital for a few weeks and was to be discharged. A local rest home was being considered because of her age, and the fact that she lived alone. Jean of course had not mentioned this to Jenna. It was by chance that Jenna heard of it and wasn't sure whether to be relieved or annoyed that she hadn't been included in the discussions. Then again, she admonished herself, why would she be? Jenna wasn't family after all. The revelation of this fact brought Jenna to the realisation that if something of a similar nature happened to her she would need to have something in place as her family were a very long way away. This in turn put her on a thought provoking journey of the who, for the what, and the possible when, scenario that no one ever does give consideration to because, things never happen 'to us' do they? They always happen to the other person. We of course are the other person in the 'to us' situation, which means things can happen to anyone, at any time. With that thought another thought ran fleeting across Jenna's mind 'there could be a book in that' which was dismissed as quickly as it had appeared because Jenna's attention had been diverted to a man being accosted in the car park two rows across from where Jenna was standing. Jenna immediately called the hospital to get Security.

Jenna had seen many things in her time, but someone accosted in a car park that was a first. Security arrived and the men were detained. Then the police arrived and Jenna was questioned. There was an arrest and the day had all too quickly run away on her.

Jenna was going to do get some Christmas treats organised for the upcoming Christmas Eve supper at the church and looking at her watch Jenna decided that perhaps she could still do that if she had a later dinner. She also thought that perhaps Jean could spend Christmas Day with her or maybe Jenna could go to where Jean was taking some Christmas cheer to her.

Nothing about Jean had been decided as yet anyway so no point getting ahead of yourself Jenna thought as she made her way to her local supermarket, taking the shopping list out of her bag she proceeded to begin her Christmas food shopping for the upcoming season and asking herself why do we go to all the fuss? Knowing that the fuss was the very things that polarised people each year. The cost. The availability, the choice, the new things.

There were lots of platters or trays done up, hampers, boxes of biscuits, brandy snaps, cakes, lollies, chocolates, and to be fair Jenna had many of those things on her list, but fancy cheese and a cracker selection is what won out in the end and Jenna had picked up a lovely cane tray at a local opportunity shop that would be perfect with some sliced fruit to complete a festive and healthy supper plate so all in all a very full day.

Jenna made herself a grilled cheese and tomato sandwich that evening for her dinner and retired quite early.

The following morning Jenna woke to a knock at the door. Getting up she called out "I'm coming" as she pulled on her brunch coat, then made her way from her bedroom, down the hallway to see who had interrupted her sleep. Opening the door she saw it was Sergeant Denton.

"Good morning Mrs. Mitchell." Jenna raised her eyebrow in mock disapproval. "Sergeant Denton. What can I do for you this morning?"

"We had a call from someone passing by your property that your fence was being painted. Did you hear anything?"

"No. I haven't asked anyone to paint my fence. This is making no sense." Jenna said trying to make some sort of order out of what she was being told.

"Do you have the person?"

"No but we have a very good description, and have matched that description to a person known to us. Mrs. Mitchell have you been digging around in places you have no need to be?"

"Whatever do you mean? Of course not, and what do you mean by known to us? Perhaps if I were to look at the fence I might be better able to assist you". Jenna said with a calmness she did not fell at all.

In very large letters were the words YOU ARE MINE BI

"I think we can all agree that the last word is incomplete, but that its meaning is there for the world to see." Jenna stated matter of factly and with a tone of disgust.

"Mrs. Mitchell have you met anyone new? Upset anyone?"

"Not to my knowledge. Perhaps it is a case of mistaken identity?" Jenna asked.

"Has anything out of the ordinary happened in the last week or so?" Sergeant Denton pressured.

"The last week or so. I have been busy, with getting Christmas bits and pieces last night after I visited Jean at the hospital. There was that business in the hospital carpark yesterday afternoon. A man was accosted and I rang for security but the police interviewed me and sent me on my way."

"Do you remember who you spoke with?"

"I have a card inside. Follow me. What can I do about the fence?"

"Nothing right at the moment but when we have finished with it, you can paint over it."

"Here it is." Jenna said handing the card over "Do you mind if I get dressed."

"Not at all. I will just make a call."

Jenna busied herself getting dressed, making her bed, putting her shoes on, and making her way to the kitchen in what seemed to her in record time. She also took two cups from the cupboard and had filled the jug turning it on before the phone call had been completed.

"I see. Yes if you would. Thank you." Sergeant Denton said concluding his call. "Mrs. Mitchell it would seem that the incident yesterday was between two rival gang members."

"And you think they are out to get me?"

"I am not sure what I think. It could well be coincidence."

"You know I do not believe in coincidence. Should I be scared something else might happen?"

"I don't know. I need to make a few more calls. Can you keep yourself busy away from the house or stay somewhere else for a few days?"

"No. I could stay at Jean's. Oh no. I think we had better check Jean's place as well."

"Jean's?"

"Jean Hazlett. I had to give her details to the Police as well, so her address is also on the paperwork."

"Are you sure you didn't talk to anyone?"

"I spoke to the Security guard and the Police and only them. Let me go to Jean's if anything is amiss I will phone you."

"No I will go."

"I will follow you then. I need to be sure things there are all right. Jean doesn't need anything else on her plate right now." Jenna said as she took her keys and walked through to the garage where her car was neatly parked as always.

Pulling up behind the police car at Jean's place it was very obvious to both of them that things were very wrong indeed. The front door was smashed and there was the familiar red paint dripped up the stairs.

"I will make a call. You stay here."

"The only people that had the addresses were the police. That is very alarming." Jenna said.

From then on the day progressed with more questions being asked than answered, and a growing disquiet in Jenna's stomach.

Jenna rang the local glazier who secured the front door. Jenna found herself once again cleaning up a chaotic scene in Jean's home and then made her way to the hospital to assure jean everything was all right. The only unresolved issue was the red paint that was on the steps. The glazier was quite sure it could be removed by using thinners and he was going to speak to someone he knew about that.

So much for Christmas cheer Jenna thought as she looked at the crest fallen face of her friend. "It makes no sense to me Jenna. None whatsoever. If I hadn't climbed up to get the beetroot none of this would have happened."

"There is no point in going there Jean. It is just broken glass and paint. No more than that I am sure."

"You are not sure at all and you shouldn't be. You might be in danger. For that matter we might be in danger."

Jenna looked out the window finding herself making a choice between consoling her friend and lying to herself. She chose to remain silent with the merest line of worry travelling across her forehead.

Jenna left for her home at around three o'clock and just before four o'clock heard a knock on her front door.

Jenna called out "Who is it?" and the reply was "Sergeant Denton." Had Jenna waited and looked out of her front window as she normally did there would have been no need to ask. The Police car was clearly parked on the driveway.

"More questions?" Jenna asked as she opened the door.

"No. Another arrest and some answers for you. Really I do not know how you do it?"

"Do what?"

"Get yourself involved in other people's business."

"What people?" Jenna asked

"The wrong kind Mrs Mitchell." Sergeant Denton answered.

Everything that had occurred had happened as a direct result of the car park incident. The Security Guard had been arrested for damaging the two properties and had appeared in court that very afternoon and pleaded guilty to wilful damage. He had also given information on what was happening in the car park which was to prove useful in an ongoing investigation.

"So thankfully you will now be fine."

"Why did he think he needed to threaten me?"

"He told us he needed to show his loyalty."

"I don't think I will ever go into that car park again."

"The truth is Mrs. Mitchell on the street, in a driveway, a car park, a shopping mall, outside a school. Clandestine behaviour is ever present right under our noses, but we seldom see it because we are not expecting it be there."

"You mean 'we' the public." Jenna said.

"Yes. I hope you don't mind but I have spoken to a painter I know and he is going to begin to restore your fence for you."

"No I don't mind. That was one of the things I was going to change actually the fence. It just doesn't look quite right." Jenna was saying when a man in overalls walked up her drive.

"Hello Paul. Mrs. Mitchell. I am Pete the painter. Are you happy for me to have a look?"

"Well it's on show for anyone passing to see. I am interested in your suggestions on how to fix it." Jenna said.

"I think a dark stain or dark paint would look good." Paul said as he was stepping into his car prior to his leaving.

"Given the trees around it I tend to agree." Pete said.

""Right then. How much will it be?"

"Nothing to you. The cost has been covered, and I will be looking at Mrs Hazlett's steps and her carpet. I believe you have a key for there. If we could go around there."

"Yes of course. I will get my things. How long will these jobs take and who covered the cost?"

"Not too long. I will get one of my men around tomorrow to start on yours. As soon as I give the quote to the police I am paid."

"Thank you. There is no urgency. I can wait." Jenna said.

"I have a postponement so in a way it has helped me out. I like to keep us busy until we close for the year."

The resolution for Jean's home wasn't quite so straight forward, but fortunately the insurance company agreed to cover the replacement of the carpet and Jenna was able to get the information for them from Jean. The paint on the stairs was removed, and the stairs looked almost like new.

Jean was transferred to the Rest Home and by the time she returned home the carpet would be replaced and things would be in order once again.

As for Jenna having a dark fence took some getting used to, but Jenna did see the benefits of the darker colour blending in with the foliage around it much better. White or light brown fences had been her normal colours up until now. Funny how unexpected events can change the colour palate of your world Jenna thought as she drove into her garage.

KAREN PIVOTT

CHAPTER THIRTEEN

It was well into January before Jean returned home, and when she did she felt very much at home.

"Jenna I can't thank you enough for all you have done. How you got the carpet replaced so quickly."

"I will stop you there Jean. I didn't get the carpet replaced quickly. The insurance assessor handled all that and she was a dream to work with, and as for the other things really all I did was make a few phone calls, put out a couple of damsel in distress vouchers and people were more than happy to assist. What you can thank me for is this." Jenna said producing a freshly preserved bottle of beetroot, with a smaller jar of beetroot relish beside it.

"My beetroot?" Jean asked.

"Yes. I didn't have the heart to let them go all woody so I asked one of the Coffin Club chap's to pull them up for me while they were here removing the items from your top cupboards. Very apt I thought. The Beetroot jar started the chain of events so I let nature run its full course and end the saga as well. I found your mother's beetroot relish recipe in the back of your old cookbook. I hope you don't mind I took the half jar that always seems to be left over and had it with some ham. Very tasty."

"Sitting in that rest home I could hear Roy saying 'I told you to get another place sorted before I left you. Now can you see what I meant?' and you know Jenna as irrational as this may sound to you even with the stairs here I don't feel ready to leave. I mean I know I said I would start looking in the New Year but that was partly because I could feel and smell Roy still here and I just missed him so much. You don't think he wobbled the step ladder so I would fall off do you?"

"No Jean I certainly don't."

"It's just that I felt like he was still here. Did you feel Adam's presence like that?"

"No Jean. I was in a fog for quite some time and to be honest after the funeral I was numb and not capable of feeling anything at all for a bit and then when I did begin to feel," Jenna paused to catch her breath and think carefully about what she would say next when jean saved her by saying.

"I'm sorry Jenna, your circumstances and mine are totally different. I should learn to stay quiet."

"Now Jean let's face it that just wouldn't be you." Jenna said with a smile "Now onto practical things. There is a map with the cupboards on it on your kitchen bench so you can find where we have put things. The top cupboards are all empty and I have put a new non-slip mat in your shower for you. All that said I think I will leave you to settle in. Your dinner is in the fridge ready to be heated."

"Roast hut?"

"Of course, and there is milk and bread for you as well. I would have liked to stay a bit longer, but I have an appointment. Phone if you need anything and I mean anything. Oh and before I forget there is a brochure from St John's on a panic alarm necklace that I was given for you on one of my visits."

"I will need to thank all the people that have helped." Jean said looking around her home which had received a spring clean for her arrival home.

"As you wish. There is plenty of time for all that. Rest up. Eat and be"

"Grateful and I am Jenna. I am very grateful." Jean said finishing her sentence for her.

A few weeks had passed by when Jenna read in the court news that the Security Guard had been sentenced to 50 hours community service which took into account, his guilty plea, remorse for the victims of his actions and the compensation he voluntarily made in having the damaged property repaired. The judge went on to say that 'your actions were reactionary to an event that had nothing to do with the two elderly people your actions impacted on, and were at best misguided, at worst ill placed.'

At least Jenna now knew who had paid for the repaint of her fence, but two elderly people. Jenna did not consider herself to be elderly not at all.

Jenna was in the process of leaving her home when the phone rang. Jenna dutifully set her bag down and answered the phone on her garage wall.

"Jenna, Judy here. Just letting you know the cover is ready for you to proof. Would Thursday say two o'clock suit you?"

"That would be fine. Judy. I will see you then."

Jenna reflected on how very short the conversation was and for Judy that was saying something in itself. Perhaps Judy didn't believe in the book. No doubt she would be more forthcoming on that score on Thursday if that was the issue Jenna thought, and proceeded to go about her daily business.

It never ceased to amaze Jenna how busy her days could be. Many of her neighbours and friends said they were bored, for Jenna the word bored had no relevance in her life whatsoever.

Mrs. Sanders two doors further along the road who had made herself know to Jenna recently was often saying "How does one fill in the days? I mean there are only so many flowers to dead head and that takes no time at all really. How do you do it?" She asked.

"I write, visit friends, read, do a spot of gardening, my days just disappear. I find there are not enough hours in the day to be honest, and when I drift off for a nana nap that compounds the issue even more." Jenna stated as she continued to weed a patch of her corner garden.

"Really. Don't you want to retire?"

"Mrs. Sanders the word retirement at this stage of my life is not in my vocabulary. I mean how would I fit that in as well?" Jenna asked.

"That is when you slow down Mrs. Mitchell."

"Yes. Well how is that working for you Mrs. Sanders? And please call me Jenna."

"Thank you Jenna. I am Dorothy and I think I can see your point. I have stopped too much too soon."

"Well it is never too late to start something new, or revisit something you enjoyed doing before."

"Do you know I used to love gardening for other mum's. They worked and I was a stay at home mum."

"Dorothy they are starting a community garden up next month for one of the schools'. It was in the local paper. They are looking for volunteers."

"Yes I remember reading that article now you come to mention it. I think I still have it. I will go home right now and dig it out. Thank you." Dorothy said and made her way home with purposeful steps.

The casual visit and informal conversation reminded Jenna of a time when she was on the Parent Teacher Association and was putting forward a fundraising idea. After the meeting when some of the group stayed for a cup of tea before going home Jenna overheard one of the ladies say, "That pushy Mitchell woman why can she not just come to the meetings, agree to things, have a cup of tea and go home, but no she has to always have us doing something. I mean don't we have enough to do?"

Jenna could have taken offence at this comment but chose not to, what she chose to do instead was to speak to this lady once she had done the dishes.

"I don't think we have been introduced. I am Jenna. Jenna Mitchell. And you are?"

"Fin. Fin Parker."

"Nice to meet you Fin. I was hoping, that you might be able to come up with some time saving tips for our fundraising this year. As a committee we are required to have three fund raising events, and as you are fairly new I wondered if you had something new and different to offer?"

"Three fundraising events per year?"

"Yes. Oh I am sorry I thought Rachel would have said. Never mind. Just because we have three fundraising events as a committee to do, that doesn't mean we all do all three. We get the wider school community involved as well. Many hands make light work as the saying goes." Jenna said leaving Fin with information that had clearly been omitted from her prior to her making the decision to join the committee. The next meeting saw a more vocal response around the group with regards to fund raising ideas for the upcoming year, and Jenna was very pleased about that. Funny what your mind remembers and when it chooses to remind you of the contents of its memory stick. Jenna thought as she put the weeds into her compost bin.

Thursday came around so quickly Jenna thought she had lost a couple of days somewhere.

Sitting in Judy's office Jenna felt that something was definitely off. For one thing Judy was running late, and in all the years they had worked together Judy had never once been late.

"By any and all means I make sure I am on time for my writers. After all without writers who am I to publish?" She had said to Jenna on one occasion when Jenna was three minutes late to a scheduled meeting. That wasn't the issue really the issue was that Jenna had made the mistake of asking "Have you never been held up and late to an appointment?" And so here was Jenna waiting for Judy who was never late which was uncharacteristic of her Jenna was thinking, when her thoughts were abruptly halted as a very apologetic Judy entered the waiting area. "Jenna I really am so very sorry. Do come in."

"There is no need to apologise things happen and you have had to wait on me at times."

"And never with an understanding or forgiving heart." Judy said, which alarmed Jenna even more.

"Whatever is going on Judy?" Jenna asked.

"I am dying Jenna. I have just now been to the lawyer to put my affairs in order." Jenna felt her eyes well with tears.

"Oh Judy."

"At least I won't linger. That is a good thing. Let's not go into the details Jenna although I will say your latest book has been a great help. I have managed to plan most things and have them in place. I probably will forget something, but I won't be here to worry about it will I? Now the cover I thought something muted? Colourful?" she said producing two mock-up covers for the book.

"Judy what do you like?"

"It is for you to choose Jenna."

"No I mean what do you like. Flowers, scenery. What images give you pleasure?" Jenna asked.

"I love cherry blossom trees lining a wide path."

"That is the image we will use for the cover. It is perfect Judy. You are a genius. Can't you see the significance of it? It represents life at its fullest, and the pathway ahead. Certainly better than either of those two." Jenna said pointing to the mock-up covers on the table.

"Oh Jenna. Thank you." Judy said. "I will get right onto it."

"Judy if there is anything at all I can do. You only have to ask."

"Well there is actually. I would like you to work on another non-fiction book. Something along the lines of living longer and enjoying it, for those who are left behind, after their loved ones have passed. The next stage for the bereaved."

"Living Longer after your loved one has passed?"

"No Jenna. 'Living Longer'. That's to be the title and maybe we could use the cherry blossoms in bloom on that cover and the cherry blossoms starting to bud for this cover. What do you think?"

"I think I will leave the covers to you and I will get on writing the book." Jenna said and gave Judy a hug before she left.

Jenna knew that it would not be Judy who published her next book, but what Jenna hadn't anticipated was how quickly she would be standing next to Tania, at Judy's funeral service or that

Judy's husband Trent would speak to her about how helpful he had found her latest book "Dying Longer". The main reason for that was simply that Jenna never knew that Judy had a husband.

Tania knew but had never met the husband, in fact not many people had. They had led professionally very separate lives and that had spilled over into their personal lives as well.

Trent made it all clear in his speech "We made the enormous mistake of believing that we had our retirement years to live and laugh together in great comfort. I will forever be sorry that we didn't get to experience that part of our lives. My life will go on much the same as before and that is not what we had agreed to. Such is life. For those of you who have partners, live together now, and if you are late from time to time, so long as you get there that is the important thing. Arriving by any and all means, means that sometimes we have to change our plans. I will miss you my darling. My successful darling."

Jenna heard stifled sobs around her and realised her own cheeks were quite wet.

CHAPTER FOURTEEN

The months had flown by and Jenna found herself busy with her next book. Writing and meetings with Tania were on track and everyone was getting used to the new publisher who had a very relaxed demeanour, but with quite an authoritative tone, which Jenna found disconcerting.

Taking all of that into account though he seemed to be very productive and appeared to be quite accommodating to his staff.

Brandon Taylor was a man to watch. Jenna suspected he would progress from this Publishing House to a much larger one quite quickly. He literally smelt of ambition, definitely dressed for it, and carried himself with confidence in a way that was almost hypnotic. In his presence you felt his success would, well drip onto you, which in reality was ridiculous because as Tania said at their scheduled meeting earlier that month "It is your success that we must not forget. You know for all Judy's crispness and no nonsense approach she acknowledged the success of her writers. Without them we are nothing, she would say, and once you forget that you are an ineffectual publisher. Having said that it is up to us the publisher to get the books out there by any and all means, even if we rattle our writer from time to time. We are a team Tania. A team where all parts must work together all the time to get the result."

With a smile Jenna had said "I take it you received that speech more than once?"

"It was shall we say rolled out regularly." Tania said with a giggle.

"You do realise that Mr. Brendon Taylor is a showman. He is doing just enough to get to the next level. He won't be with us for long. He has already dumped two writers to show he is in charge, and in my opinion he dumped the wrong two."

"Would you rather he dumped an old girl like me?" Jenna asked.

"Oh he wouldn't do that. No, no, he needs your book to propel him onto better things."

"Tania it may not do well."

"Jenna your 'Dying Longer' has done extremely well, and its sequel will match or better it."

"Your faith in me never waivers Tania."

"Neither did Judy's."

"I get the distinct feeling that you don't like Mr. Brendon Taylor very much."

"It is more that I don't trust Mr. Brendon Taylor. The Mr. Taylor you see on display is not the Mr. Taylor we see when writers are not in the building and his interpretation of 'By Any and All Means' is entirely different to Judy's, that's all I will say on that score. Of course I could be wrong. There are people who don't respond well to change and I may be one of those." Tania said with a tone of resignation, but Jenna highly doubted that was the case.

Odd to recall that conversation now Jenna thought as she was diligently working on her current chapter. Jenna was lost in her words when she thought she heard a knock on the door, pausing a moment she heard another knock a louder knock. Saving her work she left her writing room to answer the door and was greeted by Dorothy her neighbour who on this occasion was very well dressed.

"Good morning Jenna. I am so sorry to bother you. It's embarrassing really. Well I thought it was."

"Dorothy come in."

"Oh yes thank you Jenna." She said as she stepped into the foyer. "Did you hear anything unusual in the night?" Dorothy asked her.

"No I can't say I did."

"No vehicles about or people?"

"Not that I know of. Dorothy whatever is going on? You look as if you are on your way somewhere?"

"I was. That's when it started. Oh dear I am rambling. Me of all people."

"Come into the lounge and have a seat. Would you like a tea, coffee?"

"No thank you Jenna. I think I need to start at the beginning to get my mind in order." Dorothy said. Jenna sat next to her "Take your time. Now where are you going?"

"Oh yes. I was getting into the car and went to start it and it was dead. There was nothing. So I popped the bonnet to check the battery leads and well there was no battery."

"Where was your car?"

"In the garage."

"I see" said Jenna feeling some disquiet. "Anything else amiss?"

"I don't think so. I've rung the garage and they are sending a chap with a replacement battery."

"And you didn't hear anything?"

"No. I was out until quite late. I was picked up and dropped off."

"Have you rung the police?"

"For a battery? No they are busy catching criminals Jenna."

"Is anything here out of place?"

"To be honest I wouldn't know. I got up had my breakfast and started writing. I tend to go into a world of my own when that happens I'm afraid. Do you need a ride?"

"Oh no. I have plenty of time. I had better get home the young lad will be there soon. Check your garage Jenna." Dorothy said as she stood and let herself out through the front door.

Jenna did check her garage, the outside of her home, and the laundry but nothing had been disturbed, but then Jenna was further back from the road. Given what had happened Jenna thought she would check on her next door neighbour who was on vacation. Acting on her thoughts she left for their property and on her arrival there found the garage open with the door damaged but up, petrol cans missing and the car gone. Jenna phoned the Police and was told to secure the garage as best she could. Alas this was not possible as the door was too damaged for her to pull it down.

She went home and waited for the Police to contact her.

She was phoned and asked to meet them at four o'clock that day which she did.

Constable Fraser attended the call and asked Jenna a lot of questions to which Jenna replied honestly and as succinctly as possible.

Constable Fraser made the point and not for the first time "You don't know that there were petrol cans taken do you?"

"Constable let me put it to you this way. How many lawn mowers do you see?"

"Two. A ride on and a push mower."

"Next to the push mower there stands a twenty litre and a smaller Petrol can. How many Petrol Cans do you see?"

"None."

"How likely do you think it is that a person would have two mowers and no petrol cans?" So engaged was Jenna in defending her position she hadn't heard the arrival of two other Police Officers. One of whom was getting busy with the fingerprint kit.

"Mrs. Mitchell."

"Sergeant Denton. I was just trying to explain to your Constable Fraser here that Petrol Cans have been taken."

"Yes it does appear that the gap next to the push mower is the right size for a couple of Petrol Cans." He said and winked at Jenna.

"Anything else taken?"

"Apart from the car and the Petrol Cans? I wouldn't know I didn't go through to the house. There are no windows broken and the internal door seems to be untouched. There was the break in next door at Dorothy Sanders. The battery from her car was removed."

"Did she tell us about that?"

"I don't know. I told her to." Jenna said.

"Graham Brown why do I know that name? Oh yes he is a mechanic. Owned the garage on the corner of our street for a time. A time before you lived here Mrs. Mitchell. I would hazard a guess that he takes the battery out of his car when he goes away."

"Constable would you go next door and have a word with Mrs. Sanders. Do you have contact details for the Brown's?"

"Yes I have given them to your Constable Fraser. I do have a spare copy if you're interested?"

"Of course you do, and yes I am."

"I have notified their insurance company and they are sending someone to secure the garage once you have finished here."

"I think we have finished here for now." He said looking over at the officer who was packing up his bits and pieces.

"Good I will make a call then."
Jenna said dialling the company that the
Insurance people had ready to secure the
property.

"Nothing amiss at your place?"

"Thankfully no." Jenna answered
him.

"Right. We will be in touch with the
Brown's and we will also be on the lookout
for their car. How known was it that the
Brown's would be away?"

"Apart from me and their family I
couldn't say. Do you think it is someone
they know?"

"At this stage I have no idea. Lock
yourself in Mrs. Mitchell."

"Always." Jenna replied. Sergeant
Denton and the other Police Officer left. A
builders van arrived and two builders
began trying to secure the garage. Shortly
thereafter Constable Fraser made a timely
appearance as another pair of hands was
required to hold the damaged door down
while it was straightened out before it was
able to be secured into place.

Then almost as quickly as the saga
had begun it ended. As Jenna made her
way home she glanced at her watch and
saw that over ninety minutes had passed.

No wonder there is a chill in the air and the day is drawing in she thought.

On her arrival home the phone was ringing and it was Graham Brown who said "Hello Jenna. Thank you so much for taking care of everything. Anymore news?"

"Not yet. I have sent you an email through from your insurance company. You have probably received it already, but just for my peace of mind while you are away what I get from them I will forward onto you. The garage door has been secured but is, to all intent and purposes unusable in its current state, so that will be replaced. They will probably wait on your return for that, and still no word on the whereabouts of the car or the Petrol Cans. Apart from that everything else is fine by the looks of things."

CHAPTER FIFTEEN

The last chapter of the book 'Living On' was with Tania who agreed the new name was much more fitting and was very apt given that Judy herself would have realised the change would mean the book title would be more in keeping with 'Dying Longer'.

The Brown's had returned home. Their replacement garage door had been fitted, and they were discussing their replacement vehicle, when Anne heard there had been a fatal car crash in Wellington.

"Not another one. That is all we have heard since we got back. The road toll is very high this year." Anne said as she put the last of the dishes into the cupboard.

Indeed that had become all too common news, between young people who were too young to have a licence and shouldn't be driving, to older people who had medical events, tourists driving on the road side of the road, intoxicated people it wasn't just Anne Brown who was talking about it. "All this talk of the road toll and accidents on the news and none of that helps the grieving families, or the insurance premiums people are paying, or the beds taken up in the hospitals. It is depressing isn't it Mrs. Mitchell?" Sally asked as Jenna was paying her rates bill.

"Do you know Sally sometimes it is better not to know what is happening, on the hour, every hour? My husband Adam only ever listened to the news once a day to be informed, he never allowed the news cycle to inundate him with events over which he had no control."

"Do you still listen to the news once a day?" Sally asked.

"Me. Oh heavens no. There are days I never have the news on at all. I am too busy with other things."

"Like your writing?"

"Well yes Sally. Too be honest though I am in another world entirely when I am writing. Well enough chatting I have a lunch engagement today."

"Anyone I know?" Sally asked with a mischievous smile.

"Yes. Jean Hazlett."

"Well you say hello to her from me. How is she now?"

"Just back from a belated and somewhat extended holiday. I daresay I will know more by the end of our lunch time together." And with a briskness to her step Jenna was on her way to Jean's. No roast hut lunch today though, Jenna had purchased buns, coleslaw, ham and fruit from the supermarket, to go with the beetroot, cucumber, and tomatoes Jean had at home.

Jenna was surprised at how much she was looking forward to this lunch visit. She had missed Jean while she was away of course, but then Jenna had not only been busy with her book, she had also dealt with the odd distraction. Yes she would at least have some news to share with Jean about the happenings while she had been away. With a smile on her face, and a small Chill-Bag in her hand she made her way up Jean's steps and was greeted warmly. The conversation flowed well before any food had been eaten and continued throughout lunch, as well as the clearing up phase involving the dishes being loaded into the dishwasher, the table cleared and the tea being made, they took their cups of tea through to the lounge and the conversation turned to Jean and Roy's friends Cyril and Joy.

"Oh yes Roy knew Cyril in their army days. They fought in Korea together."

"Korea. That's a war we never hear much about now I come to think of it."

"So of course when Roy and I became a couple I inherited Cyril and Joy as friends to, and they have been great friends. Over the years they have stayed with us and vice-versa of course. Jenna I wasn't sure when would be a good time to tell you so I will just say it. I have found my new place. In fact I have bought my new place."

"Oh Jean I am so pleased for you." Jenna said looking at Jean who did not look very pleased at all. "Are you excited?" Jenna asked.

"I think I have made a mistake to be honest. I mean while I was there it all just happened. Well not just happened."

"Take a moment Jean and 'Let's start at the very beginning' to quote a line from the Sound of Music which seems most appropriate right now."

"I was staying with Cyril and Joy at their home on the Kapiti Coast. It is lovely there so peaceful. I knew they were building a place in Hastings in one of those new housing developments. Anyway while I was there they got a call to go up and choose their drapes, carpet and what not. I was pleased for them and said I would make my way home, but they insisted we go up together and I suppose you could say I got swept along. We went to the house and looked at the progress, then they had their input on the colour scheme, and they started looking at the grounds, and asked if I would put my plant knowledge to work there.

I made a plan and we set about looking at what the nurseries had in stock and what they could get. We placed an order with one, and anyway at the edge of the development was this house. The property is larger than the others and the house looked completely finished. I asked the builder when the new owners were going to shift in and he told me that he had no idea because that house wasn't part of the development. The section had been purchased some time before, and the house was built by a couple, but had been empty for well over twelve months. He did have the contact details in his truck which he gave me, and I rang the number and found myself talking to a man named Trevor who offered to let me have a look through the place that afternoon. Cyril and Joy were off to an appointment that afternoon so I took myself off to meet up with Trevor. From the moment I walked in I fell in love with it. He gave me the details of their lawyer having explained the situation and left me to it basically.

I contacted the lawyer, made an offer, and the family accepted it. So I then contacted my lawyer and in four weeks I can shift in. Only now Jenna it seems a rather rash thing to have done."

"Why was it for sale?"

"That's just it. I had no idea it was for sale and it is a very sad story really. Trevor's parents had the house built for their golden years only they died before it was finished within just a few days of each other, and the family have been waiting for probate. It was to be listed the following month for sale and along came Jean."

"What did you like about it? What drew you to it?" Jenna asked.

"It just struck me as a place Roy would love. A nice large house on a section that was in proportion to it. The thing is that in the development the houses are three and four bedrooms, but the section around the house is as Roy would say 'not big enough to swing a cat', where by comparison this place is. You know how you have told me houses find people and I have scoffed at you. I am rethinking that now."

"I bet you are. Do you have to sell this place right away? Could you keep this as an investment perhaps? Put people in it in the meantime?"

"I could, but that would be a hassle. I am just not sure if I should have bought the Hastings place." Jean said beginning to get tearful as she looked around her lounge.

"How far away are Cyril and Joy from you?" Jenna asked.

"Oh about five houses along I think. I haven't counted to be honest."

"They must be pleased you are going to be close by."

"Yes they are. Jenna I think I have got myself into a conundrum."

"Look." Jenna said rifling through her handbag, "Yes here it is. Pass me the phone would you Jean. Thank you." Jenna said as she was busy dialling. "Steve? Jenna Mitchell. Fine thank you. No not me. I have a friend who is in need of a property appraisal with a view to selling of course. Can you. That would be great. See you then. The address oh yes that would be useful. Jean Hazlett" and with the details given Jenna handed the phone back to Jean. "Three thirty. He has had a viewing postponed." Jenna said.

"Well I will have time to do a quick vacuum in the morning then." Jean said.

"Today Jean. He is coming today. You will like him he is a very personable young man, efficient and thorough. In forty eight hours all your doubts could have gone away."

"Forty eight hours really Jenna that is most unlikely."

"Stranger things have happened." Replied Jenna acknowledging quietly to herself that forty eight hours may be an optimistic time frame even by her standards, but as it eventuated even Jenna was taken by surprise at how things turned out.

Steve and his team of Real Estate Agents arrived and walked through the house and around the grounds and while they were there Steve made a phone call. Jenna left Jean to the paperwork and made her way home, and was just finishing up her additional piece for the book she had thought was finished, having emailed it through to Tania when the phone rang.

"Jenna you won't believe what has happened. Steve brought a couple around and they have made me an offer. A good offer."

"Well Jean there is your answer. Things have been put in place for all to be well. Are you going to accept the offer?"

"I have accepted the offer. I will be in need of your contact list for my relocation."

"I am happy to help. You did say there were plenty of rooms available in Hastings?"

"There will always be a room for you Jenna." Jean said sounded excited which pleased Jenna. Meant to be she thought as she closed her computer down for the day and made her way to the kitchen for a very welcome cup of herbal tea.

Just as she had taken the tea bag out of her cup, she was interrupted by a knock on her front door.

Leaving her cup she went to the door and opened it to find her neighbours Graham and Anne standing there holding a box of chocolates and a bunch of flowers.

"What on earth?" Jenna asked.

"Just a small token of our appreciation for what you did. Nothing to get too excited about." Graham said.

"Would you like a cup of tea or coffee? I have just this minute brewed myself a cup." And with that the Brown's followed Jenna into the lounge and Jenna went into the kitchen to make two cups of coffee their beverage of choice on this occasion.

Handing them their drinks, Graham began bringing Jenna up to speed with the events of the day. "We got a call from Constable Fraser around eleven this morning wasn't it Anne? Telling us they had found our car. Burned to a crisp."

"You do exaggerate he said burned out." Anne corrected him.

"We are speaking with a writer. Burned to a crisp sounds much better don't you agree? And to be honest while we are on the writing thing. When we heard we were getting a writer for a neighbour I was somewhat displeased. I had connotations of a hippy or some such shifting in. You know the alternative lifestyle creeping in. Yes well Anne soon put me right on that front didn't you Anne?"

"I am so sorry Jenna. He has had a couple."

"And what is wrong with a couple?" There was no response to that question and Jenna could see by the embarrassed look on Anne's face that it had probably been more than a couple and that perhaps the coffee Jenna had served could have been considerably stronger. The conversation soon returned to the car and the replacement car and then they were once again on their way.

A day of closures and new beginnings Jenna mused as she tidied up the kitchen. "What will tomorrow bring us?" She asked the hat as she walked passed, knowing the hat always had the perfect answer. There was never any argument from the hat.

CHAPTER SIXTEEN

Jean's shift had gone well and Jenna had met Joy who had come up to drive Jean down to Hastings. The plan was they were to leave just after the truck so they would be there in a timely manner for the unloading phase as well. And as with many well laid out plans things didn't go smoothly, with Cyril suggesting he stay behind in case there was a delay worked out perfectly. The truck was met and by the time jean and Joy arrived most of the hard work had been done, so everyone was happy with the outcome.

It still surprised Jenna that Jean didn't drive. Jean had had no need to of course, her husbands had done the driving and she had always walked most places. Before Jean sold the car Jenna had asked her if she wanted to keep it in case she needed someone to drive her somewhere, but she said no so emphatically that Jenna thought on that occasion that she may have over stepped a boundary, all be it one she hadn't seen.

So life without Jean, a new book heading for the book stores and the family waiting on news of Jenna's next visit to them.

Jenna chose to go after the next Christmas and spend time with each one as she had previously. Not with Jason this time though. Jason was coming home from Harvard for Christmas this year and he and Eden had invited Jenna to spend Christmas day with them.

Surprisingly all Jenna's family thought that was a great idea, whether they were being polite or just pleased Jenna had travel dates sorted to see them she wasn't sure, but it seemed to Jenna that the time was right at last for a quiet Christmas, which was not that far away.

This year Jenna decided to give her grandchildren money to buy what they wanted, and she thought she would give her children money for a night out.

Having decided on that she made a note so she would get the money to them in good time.

September already, the year was moving along quite quickly. I will be with Jean next month and that will be here before I know it as well, and it was with that thought, interrupted by the phone ringing, that Jenna found herself talking with Brendon Taylor, who was advising her that he had arranged for her to do some book signings, starting in two weeks and in book stores in Auckland, Whangarei, Hamilton, Wellington, Christchurch and some other places yet to be confirmed around the country. This was completely unexpected. Jenna had never been keen on doing book signings. Brendon assured her all would be arranged. "All I need you to do is turn up and make sure your writing hand is working well. That's it. I will do the rest."

It had been many years since Jenna had been expected to do a book signing, but there you have it she thought. A new publisher revisiting an old marketing strategy perhaps? Regardless of the why Jenna now had to get her head around the upcoming book signing, and working out what easy care clothing she would be best to take. Then there was the mail to be held at the post office until she returned. Bills to pay ahead of time so they didn't incur a late fee, if Jenna was away on the due date, and then Jenna had a thought of her own and phoned Brendon back. "Would it be possible to have a book signing in Hastings just before Labour Weekend? It's just I am going to be staying there anyway and it may be an opportunity."

"Well I had you going to Napier mid-October so I could push that back and you could do two book signings instead of one. How does that work for you?"

"I will make it work. Thank you Brendon. May I ask who will be coming with me?"

"I have arranged for Tania to be with you and take care of all the arrangements. It is not an Editor's job, but then we are all hands to the pump around here at present. No need for you to worry about that. She will meet you at each store. I will send through the itinerary."

As soon as that phone call ended Jenna phoned Tania.

"Tania. It's Jenna. I understand you are to accompany me on the book signing trip, and I am wondering how you feel about that?"

"It doesn't matter how I feel about it Jenna that is what is happening. Bas has been great about it, and very pleased you are the author of choice."

"I want you to know you can say no Tania. Don't agree to it just because of some sense of misplaced loyalty to me."

"My sense of loyalty to you is not misplaced. At the end of the day Barbara is the person who would normally do the book signing trips, but she is no longer with us." Tania said.

"Oh. I thought it was Craig. I must be mistaken."

"No it was Craig, but he left. Barbara was the new Craig and"

"Now she has left to. I see", Jenna said "We will have some catching up to do on this trip then?"

"I may not be with you at every store, but I will have everything set up and ready for you. We will see how it goes."

"Yes I see. We will make it work between us Tania. It has been some years since I did a book signing, but I daresay it hasn't changed all that much."

"See you in Auckland then." Tania said just before she ended the call.

Jenna did not have to be a psychic to work out that things were not going that well at the Publishing House. So concerned was she about this that she mentioned it to Vincent her son in Canada.

"Mum, clearly your publisher thinks the book signing is the right option to bring a higher profile for your book, and before you say it, I know you never did enjoy the book signings when we were younger, but you handled them then, and you will manage these ones perfectly well also."

Brittany joined the conversation and added "He is such a man. All he heard was the book signing where as I heard your concern about the state of the publishing house under the new publisher Brendon. Am I right?"

"Absolutely right." Jenna said with a smile.

"Well in that case" Vincent said "I would make the very best of the book signings, and look for a new publisher if you intend to write any more books, or pray for a replacement that brings better people skills with them to the publishing house."

"I never said he had bad people skills." Jenna said.

"He is going through reliable staff hand over fist I bet, and that usually means poor people skills."

"Or that people don't like the changes he is putting in place?"

"Let's agree one or the other or a combination of both. Listen to your gut it hasn't let you down over the years I've known you." Brittany said.

Jenna found comfort with the support of her daughter in law. Yes Vincent had expressed his input a very late save in the conversation from Jenna's point of view, but Brittany was right Jenna had a very uneasy feeling in the pit of her stomach.

The Brown's agreed to keep an eye on Jenna's home while she was away, and Jenna explained she would be away intermittently over the coming weeks. "The week after labour Weekend things will be back to normal." Jenna told Anne.

"It is so exciting a book signing." Anne had said.

"Yes they bring surprises with them as well if my memory serves me correctly." Jenna replied as she took her leave of them.

Two weeks literally flew by, and Jenna found herself sitting at the table provided covered with books for her to sign. The doors opened at precisely nine o'clock and people began lining up at her table. Tania looked over at her and winked. Where the next three hours went neither of them knew, but Tania found herself having to get more books for her to sign.

"Well that was a surprise. I mean I know these books are proving popular." Tania was saying when Jenna interrupted "I wasn't expecting them to bring the Dying Longer book with them to be signed as well." As she stretched her fingers.

Tania left for the next book store across the shore and Jenna followed her a little later. With book signing number two finished the pair made their way to their Motel and walked to a local café for a light dinner.

"You have signed and sold more books today than I was prepared for. I have phoned ahead to get more books delivered for the book signing tomorrow afternoon. If we leave around eight o'clock in the morning will that be all right with you?" Tania asked.

"Yes that will be fine. I will be able to help you set up." Jenna said.

"Thank you."

"Tomorrow may be a lot less busy than today."

"Let us hope so. My fingers were cramping today. Remind me to get some Magnesium tablets in the morning will you?"

'Magnesium Tablets?"

"Yes they work a treat every time. I am sure we will have time to stop at a Chemist or a Supermarket before the afternoon signing session begins."

"We will make time." Tania said. "I am going to have dessert will you have some too?"

"Not for me. You go right ahead and enjoy. I may have an Iced Chocolate though. I haven't had one of those since Richard and Stephanie shifted."

"Time passes doesn't it Jenna?"

"All too quickly." Jenna agreed.

Throughout the book signing trips Jenna got to meet people who had read her earlier books, all aging as she was. Many people were buying the two books for family members and friends. The days were long, the nights filled with great conversation and lots of laughter with Tania. Her children were a good source of amusement on any given day, and they brought back memories of Jenna's own children as they grew up. Their bumps and scrapes. Their unceremonious landings at times made all the more memorable by where they landed. Yes Jenna admitted this book signing trip was a success on more than the marketing side of the business.

Tania and Jenna said their goodbyes in Hastings. Jenna had driven to Napier in her car separately from Tania knowing she would be staying on. The book signing in Napier was very busy in the morning and the afternoon book signing in Hastings was quite busy too. Although it ran over time Jenna was pleased to be able to leave for Jean's at the respectable hour of four o'clock. Having found her way to the right street Jenna was then able to find the house. As soon as Jenna drove into the driveway she knew exactly why Jean had fallen in love with the house and grounds, they shouted Roy, from the shape of the house, to the layout of the garage and the built in shelving. This was exactly the home Roy had described for Jean. Jenna parked her car into the opened garage and Jean appeared like magic on the scene.

"What do you think?"

"I think. No. I know. Roy would have loved it Jean."

"Wait until you see the rest then." Jean said with a look of excitement on her face.

CHAPTER SEVENTEEN

It was exactly as Jenna had surmised, right down to the two toilets, two bathrooms, separate office, large bedrooms, large kitchen, separate dining room, two living areas, separate laundry, internal access to the garage, large grounds, it was as if Roy had been the architect and builder sent in advance to make the perfect home for his beloved.

It gave Jenna warm fuzzies and goose bumps all at the same time.

Enjoying their dinner together after the grand tour had concluded for the day, and Jenna had put her clothes away in her room, Jenna reached over to give Jean a copy of her book, 'Living On' saying " I will sign it for you of course."

"Jenna you don't need to give me one I have bought one and read it already, and I am touched, truly touched by the dedication."

"Well Jean I felt it was right. You and Roy inspired the first book 'Dying Longer'. Your selfless access meant that a true account of all that was involved could be shared with others, and you have gone on 'Lived On' as you both committed to." Jenna said.

"Is that why you changed the name of the book?"

"Partly, and partly because Living Longer just didn't feel quite right somehow." Jenna said.

"Well perhaps you can send my copy to Judy's widower with a personalised notation. You will have done that already I suppose." Jean said.

"Actually Jean I haven't and how remiss of me. I will put it in the post for him tomorrow. I have my laptop with me so I will look up his address. Do you know Jean I worked with Judy on an off for over twenty years and I don't think I knew her at all."

"I think you did Jenna. You knew the publisher. It was in that capacity that your relationship was formed and flourished.”

“I hadn’t thought about it like that.”

“You do realise don’t you that you helped make her a successful publisher. Your books have sold more than any of their other writers.”

“No I didn’t know that.” Jenna said surprised on two fronts. One that Jean had found that information out in the first place and two that Jenna herself had never bothered to gauge her success in quite that way.

The following morning Jean took Jenna around her grounds which had been divided into shrubbery, vegetable patch, and it came as no surprise to Jean that the vegetable patch was very large, flower beds, borders and fruit trees. Jean had ordered some large trees which were to arrive on the Tuesday.

“It could be a bit dusty, but they do everything.” Jean was saying as she showed Jenna the space the trees would be occupying. “The beauty of it is, they will give the place character and it will look as if I have been here for ages.”

“Is it expensive getting established trees brought in?”

"Well Jenna here is how I look at it. Do I have forty years left to wait for them to grow and fill the space?"

Jenna found herself looking around for her hat, but he was adorning her wall at home. The hat of course would have had the correct response for that.

"Jenna?"

Jenna smiled, "I can see a water feature here." Jenna said to deflect the earlier comment pointing to a gap where the patio ended and the border began.

Jean walked to the spot Jenna had just moved off and said, "Perfect. I was going to put a couple of large pots here and plant them up, but a water feature oh Jenna why didn't I think of that?" Jean said. "Let's do some online browsing over a cuppa and see what's on offer shall we?"

Which is exactly what they did, and Jenna found herself quite taken aback at how pragmatic Jean had become, but then Jenna remembered that Jean had been nick-named the pushy one when she was involved on church committees so maybe this was the Jean people had talked about. Jenna decided that Jean was motivated, settling in, and was at times looking happy, and that was all progress to Jenna. Progress is always a good thing if you don't always like the route it is taking she recalled someone saying not too long ago or words along those lines. It was David she remembered who had said that.

The weekend slipped by all too quickly, and the trees were installed on the Tuesday, in a timely manner, with great care and precision. The day had gone by rather quickly with the Bob Cat arriving early to dig the holes for the trees. With their job done they left a good half hour before the truck arrived with the trees, followed by a Utility Truck with two additional workers and some tools, and from that point on it was all go. The men took the trees from the truck and placed them in front of the holes where they were to go, then went over to their vehicles took their lunch boxes out and sat down.

Jenna said "I had no idea it was lunchtime already." To which Jean replied "I will put the jug on and rustle something up."

In no time the activity had begun again and Jean said "I think we will just take our time with these sandwiches Jenna."

"What and miss the trees going into their new home? Not likely." Jenna said as she put her plates and mug in the sink and made her way to the back door.

And in less than four hours the whole task was completed.

They were given a very good drink of water, and "One of our people will be along in a couple of weeks' time, to check on them. We don't envisage any issues, but we do like to keep an eye on them early in the piece."

"Yes. Thank you John." Jean said as he was climbing into his truck.

He and the other two workmen left and Jenna stood transfixed. Jean was right. They really did look as if they had been there all along. If you didn't notice the dirt that had been swept in around the trees.

"Well I must say whatever they cost you they are more than worth it." Jenna said to a smiling Jean who looked very pleased indeed.

"The water feature will be next." Jean said. "It will give me a project to do before Christmas. You are still going to spend Christmas Day with Eden and Jason?"

"Yes Jean I am and do you know it has just occurred to me that it will be the first Christmas since I was eighteen that I am doing nothing for Christmas. No food preparation, cooking, nothing at all and it is a good and somewhat sobering feeling all at once. Quite contradictory." Jenna said.

"If you are going to use large words like that around me Jenna Mitchell, I think you need to start thinking about writing another book." Jean said with a giggle.

Still feeling the effects of the book signings, writing another book wasn't in Jenna's mind at all.

Jean brought the subject up again just after dinner that evening.

"Really Jean I am not in the right frame of mind to do another book. I have done two non-fiction books back to back."

"I know but you have a readership, a following. People love your books."

"Now you are sounding like a publisher who wants a writer to write a book they are not ready to write."

"Maybe I should have been a publisher?"

"You are certainly pushy enough." Jenna said and was about to apologise when Jean said "you know Jenna I do think at times I missed my calling. Perhaps I was too busy bossing someone somewhere and didn't hear what I was meant to do in this life." Jean said which completely floored Jenna.

"New town. New opportunities. It is never too late to open yourself up to new beginnings. A new direction maybe Jean?"

"Or a new book Jenna." Jean added.

And with the very welcome sound of dodo do....dada da Jenna knew a Skype call was waiting for her to answer. Expecting it to be a family member Jenna was very surprised to see Tania address on the screen followed shortly thereafter by Tania in the flesh.

"Oh Jenna I am so very pleased you have your laptop on. I was going to wait but I just couldn't, and Bas asked me, honey why are you waiting?"

Bas standing behind Tania said "Hi Jenna has she got some news to tell you. Oh boy."

"Well I'm intrigued. Tania you remember Jean?"

"Yes hello Jean. I don't meant to be rude but I'm bursting."

"Well burst away." Jenna said,

"It's Brendon. He's been done for supplying Methamphetamine. All those meetings, and no new clients. All the travelling around on the publishing house, and all the while he was peddling drugs. I told you he wasn't the same guy around different people."

"Yes you did. What's going to happen now then?"

"Tania is going to try her hand at being a publisher." Bas said.

"No I'm not Jenna. I was asked to step in temporarily and I thought what would Jenna say and so I am asking for your advice."

"So long as you can be Tania, the nice, kind, lovely Tania with the odd shove to get writers motivated and working, I think you would be brilliant. Just one thing though you may get a taste for it."

"Publishing?"

"Shoving" Jenna said and they all laughed.

"Did you suspect anything?" Jean asked Jenna when the call had concluded.

"In my gut something felt off, but I never thought for one moment that was the reason." Jenna said and then asked Jean "How about I take you to a movie tomorrow. We will have a 'girls' day out. Perhaps Joy would like to join us?"

"Oh how very Jenna of you. Do you know Jenna I am enjoying it being just the two of us, besides on a Wednesday Cyril and Joy play Bridge, and no one, or nothing interrupts their Bridge day."

"Well then we had best see what is on and decide what movie, what session, and where we are going for a meal afterwards. Do you know I feel like a teenager?" Jenna said.

"No I don't think I want to go there." Jean responded as she went to get the local paper.

"How are you feeling Jean?" Jenna asked all gaiety now gone and being quite serious.

"I am starting to feel better. Slowly but surely, and it's early days yet. My concern is for you. This really will be your first Christmas on your own since Adam died. How are you feeling about that?"

"To be honest I'm not quite sure. Do you know it is three years since he died?

Where have they gone? I am fifty eight Jean and I have a long road of living stretching out before me, and I am not so sure what I am going to be doing. So in the grand scheme of things, this upcoming Christmas is but a blip on the horizon of the future life of Jenna Mitchell."

"Yes very well, but you haven't answered my question. Are you going to be all right Jenna?"

"Do you know I have absolutely no idea, but I told you I am not going to be on my own I will be with Eden and Jason!" Jenna reminded Jean.

"I am not talking about Christmas Day Jenna. I am talking about the Christmas season." And to that Jenna had no response because she had only focussed on the one day, so she reminded Jean "Our focus right now is on our movie tomorrow. Now what options do we have?" After a brief discussion they decided on a comedy, and that they would have lunch before the movie at home, go to the movie, then look at the shops, then have an early dinner at a Thai Restaurant.

Jenna went to bed with her thoughts focused on the next day and slept soundly.

CHAPTER EIGHTEEN

It was on the drive home the following Monday that Jenna realised she was a very fortunate woman. She had friends who were understanding, caring, welcoming and a lot of fun to be with. And Jenna had made two new friends as well. Cyril and Joy had come over to Jean's on the Thursday prior to Jenna leaving and invited Jean and Jenna to join them on an outing involving a picnic and a quiet beach. "Swimming is allowed." Cyril said "I hope you have brought your togs with you Jenna."

To which Jenna replied "Never thought of packing them."

"You do have togs don't you Jenna?" Jean asked.

"No Jean. I haven't had a pair of togs for years".

"I will find mine." Jean said. "I can't believe you have no togs Jenna."

"Well perhaps if my generous proportions were better distributed like yours Jean I would feel more comfortable about wearing them."

"If that were the case Jenna there would be a lot of men who would never feel the water again." Cyril said and they all laughed.

So they had a lovely Friday out together. Cyril and Jean swam, Joy and Jenna walked the beach collecting driftwood and shells and on the way home Cyril said "Cyril and the three J's what adventures are we having when you come back Jenna?" Which Jenna thought was lovely and knew that there would be many, and that God willing she would be going back there often.

Jean had suggested that Jenna return in mid-January and Jenna was considering that would be a very good time of year for her.

She arrived home late afternoon and had unpacked her car when she heard a knock on her door "Hello and welcome home" Anne said as Jenna opened the door to her.

"No Graham with you?" Jenna asked.

"No. Graham has had a mishap, and is recovering well in hospital."

"Oh dear. What happened?"

"There is plenty of time to tell you all about that. Tomorrow morning over a coffee perhaps say ten o'clock? That is why I popped over actually. To check you are home safe and sound and to extend the invite."

"Thank you Anne. I would love to come, and as you can see I am fine. It was a lovely drive home, not much traffic which is always a bonus." Jenna said, and Anne took her leave.

Not like Anne to invite people over Jenna thought as she busied herself with watering her indoor plants, before heading into town to get some groceries and something for dinner.

The following morning with Anne Jenna was told "Graham being Graham just wouldn't wait for someone to fix the leak and climbed up the ladder himself to clear the spouting lost his balance and when I got home he was lying in a heap on the hot concrete and had been there for some time. I was not impressed. Apart from the fact that he had a few, he didn't have a shirt on and was very badly sunburned as well. He will be in hospital for several weeks."

"Oh I see." Jenna said.

"I am glad Jenna that someone other than me does. His drinking is out of hand. I have been going to ALAC a group for family members to get support while they are living with an Alcoholic. And he is Jenna. His couple of drinks are more like six or seven, and his few are more like well you get the idea, and he gets so aggressive these days with it. I get quite uncomfortable. I mean I don't feel I can invite people over anymore he has become so rude and obnoxious, and even over there in the hospital he is asking for his nightcap. Really. I have had enough." Anne stated and Jenna could see that she was at her wits end.

"Are you finding the group helpful Anne?"

"Yes. Very. In the first instance I had my thoughts validated instead of being told by Graham constantly that I was over reacting and that there was nothing wrong with 'my' drinking. You see it is not the drink per se. It is what the person is doing with the drink. How much they are drinking. How it is affecting them. It has been a very informative experience. I have no idea what I will do when he comes home, but there will be respite care before that happens so I have time to come up with a plan. Oh Jenna I am sorry I have literally dumped three years of worry and frustration on you less than twenty four hours after your return home."

"Never mind about that. You say this happened in the last three years. Did he not drink before that?"

"Of course we did. The occasional wine, spirit, bottle of beer or cider, on a weekend, or a birthday. I still have the odd drink myself. Graham started to drink more often, and more of it.

"What happened three years ago that brought the change about?"

"Do you know Jenna I never gave that a thought. Never asked that question. A couple of things now I come to think of it. He retired three years ago. Four years later than he was going to and his best mate died that same year. His fishing mate. Yes they were going to do all sorts of things together when they retired, but Graham kept working. Do you know Jenna when I gave up work for us to enjoy our retirement years together I did so knowing that my involvement with the community groups would continue. I never thought that Graham had work, fishing and that was it. Food for thought. Well he still has the fishing but of course he hasn't gone since. Jenna you don't think there may be more to it?"

"That Anne is something you need to ask Graham, and do you really want to do that?"

"I feel I need to do something. They say there is a trigger and until that is identified. Well that is half the battle. I find myself in new territory. I sit at the meetings and I hear people talking and think yes Graham does that to. No Graham doesn't do that. There are times when I wonder if I am the one who should be at the meetings, and how much enabling I have been doing. I feel responsible for some of it. I've missed things Jenna."

"I think Anne you have realised there is an issue and you are on the road to getting support to deal with it. Let's not confuse that with you causing or creating the issue. You do not have an issue with alcohol yourself do you Anne?

"No. If anything the issue for me is I am drinking less, when drinking more may have numbed me from the issue altogether."

"Yes I see. Well let's not go there. I think you have made a good choice going to ALAC and the rest will be up to Graham. Graham will have to make his own choices." Jenna said.

"Yes." Anne agreed. "And Jenna I may not be happy to live with what they might be."

"That Anne is a conversation, and decisions for another time don't you think?"

"Yes of course. I am going over later this afternoon if you need anything in Hamilton or want to have a look at the shops while I am at the hospital I am happy to take you over."

"Thank you Anne, but I am thinking if we are going that far together perhaps I could accompany you to see Graham and then we could look at some shops together after that?"

"Really Jenna I don't know where you get your energy from." Anne said "I will be leaving at two thirty."

"Right I will come over in good time." Jenna said as she stood to leave.

Jenna had a very sinking feeling in her stomach as she left. She went home had some lunch, and took her cup of tea to her favourite chair by the window and promptly dozed off. She woke to the phone ringing and was talking with Tania when she glazed over at the clock. "I'm sorry Tania I will have to cut this call short I am supposed to be somewhere. I will phone you later." Jenna said putting the handset down, grabbing her bag and walking briskly to meet Anne who was just making her way to the car.

"There's no rush. I was just putting a few things in for Graham." She said and Jenna looking at her watch realised she had only just made it. Judy would've been impressed. From dozing to a standing start in less than two minutes. Thank you Tania, Jenna thought for your timely call.

"Right. Let's hit the road." Anne said as Jenna availed herself of the passenger seat and put her seatbelt on.

All in all the visit was a non-eventful one, due in part Anne shared "Having someone with me. Seems to have made a difference. He has been quite grumpy up until now."

"You know Anne, Graham is in a lot of pain. Spinal injuries are complicated."

"Yes. I know. Oh Jenna I have been dealing with the drinking issue. Am I doing him a dis-service?"

"No. Graham has more than the drinking issue to deal with and remember Anne he hasn't been drinking since his fall."

"Well not that we know of." Anne said pulling into a shopping mall carpark.

"I feel there is a big change coming Jenna and at my stage of life that is quite frightening." Anne said.

"Change at any time of life can be frightening or liberating depending on the circumstances, the people and the timing. Some changes can be good." Jenna said giving her hand a squeeze.

Jenna went over with Anne once sometimes twice a week to see Graham who was making very slow but steady progress. It looked as if he would be spending Christmas in respite care at a local rest home with hospital facilities and Anne seemed quite relieved about that. He may have been wanting to spend Christmas at home, but Anne wasn't comfortable with that option just yet, so she arranged to spend the whole day at the home and had started making treat bags for the residents who would be unable to go away as well.

As it happened that was not to be. Graham passed away peacefully in his sleep the following Monday night. Anne phoned Jenna who drove Anne to the hospital and after they had finished there, drove Anne directly to the local funeral director as she had requested.

"Something quick and small is all he needs. No fuss Graham. That was his nick name where he worked. No fuss. No waste is what he was known for. When he tried to retire at sixty five they said they couldn't afford to let such a thrifty fellow go. Well that's what he told me." Anne said.

Jenna went in with Anne and introduced her to Dallas Robinson the son of the owners who was part of the business.

"Hello Mrs. Mitchell." He said.

Jenna noted that prices were now on display in the catalogue all be it discreetly, and there was more discussion around options available for families which in Anne's case was not valid.

"That will not be an issue. We were the family. Just the two of us. No children. No parents or Aunts and Uncles left. The reality of being only children who had no children. A private funeral with a ", Anne paused and asked "Jenna what type of casket did you have for?"

"It is really more about what type of casket do you want him in Anne?"

"There is an inner option for cremation. We put the inner in the casket and then only the inner is used."

"Yes I see. That would appeal to Graham. As little waste as possible in all things he would say. He forgot that when it came to the drink, but then he wasn't wasting it was he? No. He was drinking it." Anne said as if she was alone with her thoughts, which of course she wasn't

Jenna asked "How soon could the service take place?"

"Oh yes. Let me see. Thursday morning ten o'clock?" he asked.

"Well that sounds good to me. We will see you then." Anne said with a finality that surprised Jenna.

"How many can we expect? And are you wanting us to take care of the catering for you?" Dallas asked.

"Sorry who are you again? I mean your name. Your name has escaped me." Gone just like that. I am so sorry."

"Dallas. Dallas Robinson. My father Timothy will join us on the day. And before you go I need details for the notice to go into the paper."

"Of course you do. Let's see his name obviously. Loved by his wife Anne. And the service details. There won't be many people to notify. Is it really necessary?" Anne asked.

"It is a legal requirement." Dallas answered.

"Of course it is. I will do the food thing. There won't be many people." Anne said. "He was quite reclusive."

"In my experience more people show up than you expect." Dallas said kindly.

On their way to the car Anne said.

"Honestly he makes it sound like an event of some sort." It is Jenna thought but didn't voice those thoughts to Anne.

"He seemed a very nice young man. Very accommodating."

"Yes. They have made changes there." Jenna said

CHAPTER NINETEEN

The funeral was attended by about thirty people which seemed to genuinely surprise Anne, most of the people offering their condolences Anne had never met or heard of before but they all seemed to know Graham extremely well. Many got up to give speeches and all of them went to the house afterwards.

Anne had organised some food, but Jenna on seeing how many had turned up ordered additional food from a local bakery, and stopped into the supermarket to get some slices, which she cut up at her home and plated up. When she arrived she had food and an extra jug.

After everyone had left and Jenna was tidying up Anne said "Thank you Jenna for the food. I had no idea. None."

"Well my experience of funerals is varied, but if there is one constant to them it is the unexpected surprises that seem to arrive with them. Mostly unannounced." And not all welcome Jenna thought.

"All those people. He must have been embarrassed by me or something."

"No I don't think it was that. There was his work world. His fishing and you."

"Jenna I didn't even know he was in a fishing club."

"Did Graham know all the clubs you are involved with?"

"I told him. Oh I see what you mean. If those people turned up he wouldn't know them either."

"Exactly. Now is there anything else you would like me to do?"

"Not just now. I am very tired all of a sudden. I think I will have a lie down."

Jenna left and drove to the local gardens where she walked around in a dazed state for a bit. Sitting on one of the seats provided she looked at the colour on display. The roses were brilliant and the scent wafted across the grounds very nicely. Jenna sat for quite some time before deciding to return home and unload her car of plates and the jug. "It's been a nice joy ride for you lot" she said as she eyed them on the back seat.

Later that evening Jenna realised that most of her friends were older than herself. This was the second funeral she had been involved with in less than a year. Time to take up a new something. Hobby? Sport? Jenna was thinking of what she would like to do when she returned from her travels in April and remembered she was supposed to phone Tania back.

"I am so sorry Tania. Things have overtaken me. I meant to get back to you before now. Judy would not be impressed with me would she?"

"Definitely not. I gathered something had come up Jenna. How is that neighbour of yours who fell off the ladder?"

"He has left this world." Jenna told her.

"Oh I see. Well that explains a lot then. Look Jenna I just wanted to ask you if you were considering writing another book."

"Really Tania? To be honest I am still recovering from the book signings."

"Really?"

"No Tania not really. I haven't had time to think about writing or much else over the last few weeks. Look you know I am away in March. Let me have a think about it. Now last time we talked you were telling me about your new Barbara, Craig."

"Celeste now, and she is wonderful. So organised and very good with just about whatever I ask her to do."

"So you are enjoying being the publisher then?"

"I am enjoying the challenge of the role Jenna yes. I don't see myself as the publisher. I am just filling in." And with that the talk resumed to the children where the original conversation was before Jenna had to end it abruptly over two weeks earlier.

The following afternoon Jenna found herself on the phone talking with Pamela Tiggs.

"You may not be aware of this Jenna but most of the people in our current group have both your books, and they all appreciate your involvement with our group, all be it one from a distance, and they have asked if you would like to come to our Christmas lunch on December fourth. You don't have to give me an answer now." Pam said.

"I would love to come. Do you think I should bring a pen? Sign a few books while I am there to earn my lunch?"

"I think they would love that."

"Right then. I will put that into my calendar and I will see you at ten thirty. Thank you Pam for asking."

"Don't thank me it was their idea. To be honest I thought you would decline the invitation."

"Perhaps it is time I started being a little more visible again." Jenna said.

"Way past time if you ask me." Pam said as she ended the call.

"So," Jenna said to the hat, "this is the Christmas Season stuff Jean was concerned about. What to do if I get more invitations?"

The hat as ever was non-committal. "You," Jenna said sternly "are no help whatsoever." Tapping the edge of the hat as she walked by.

November one of Jenna's favourite months glided along without incidents, or emergencies, or any great happenings at all which Jenna was finding very restful. All the children were doing well.   The grandchildren were doing well, Jean was in touch by phone weekly and keeping Jenna up to date with the Water Feature project, and going over plans for when Jenna would be staying with her in mid-January "for a couple of weeks at least please?" Jean asked "The weather will be settled, and Cyril and Joy are so looking forward to our outings. Cyril says while we can, we should."

"Well Cyril has retired, and I am well to be honest I don't quite know what I am these days. I have decided to be more visible next year, attend meetings and groups I have been supporting from behind the scenes. So I will have to see. At this stage you are scheduled in Jean for two weeks. And there is that book you and Tania keep banging on about. I have no idea what that will be about so that is taking up some thinking time." Jenna said. But the truth of it Jenna acknowledged to herself was that two weeks away in January would be quite enough. And not for the first time Jenna reminded herself that she was younger and still very active in her whatever it was cycle of life. Some would say she was privileged. Some might say she was semi-retired. Others just called her the widow who didn't have to work. The truth of it was that there are all kinds of work. Paid. Unpaid. Voluntary. Jenna had a foot in all those camps, and was blessed with having the bulk of her money working for her freeing up her options, choices, and availability in service to others. Next year Jenna decided she would add some rest and recreation and fun things she would like to do for Jenna Mitchell. Still having absolutely no idea what they may be, she wrote in her journal the need to do something new and schedule it into her week.

With that thought in mind Jenna pressed on with her day. It was now just passed the half-way point of November. Jenna had transferred the Christmas money to her children and grandchildren so they had the money while the exchange rate was more optimal for them. Being more optimal for them meant of course that it was less optimal for Jenna, but then these were gifts and Jenna had always believed that when you gave a gift it should be given with love, and Jenna also knew that teenagers could make and extra dollar or two go a very long way indeed.

As noble as all this may seem Jenna thought as she locked her front door I have just got another thing done and out of my head.

Jenna was on her way to see Dorothy her neighbour two doors down. Dorothy had phoned and asked Jenna to help her with something "It won't take long and there is no rush." Dorothy had said over the phone.

So Jenna walked along and knocked on Dorothy's front door and was greeted warmly. "Thank you Jenna. I know how busy you are. I do appreciate your coming. Follow me." She said in a commanding tone which surprised Jenna, and Jenna dutifully followed Dorothy through the house and into the back yard.

"It's these solar lights. You see and I can't seem to work out how they go. I bought them to go along the fence but no matter how I try. Well it's not working." Dorothy said with a tone of utter exasperation. "You see here the chords, leads, whatever they call them are just not long enough."

"Yes Dorothy I see. Do you have the box?"

"Yes of course I will just get it."

Having ascertained there was no actual instruction sheet with the lights, Jenna looked at the picture on the box and informed Dorothy that she had purchased Solar lights that go in a circular pattern around a tree.

"Oh I see." Dorothy said and undeterred added "Given how many there are I think we best find a big tree then and put them to work there." Standing up and walking around to the front of the house Dorothy decided on the tree nearest the front door and in no time at all the solar lights were installed and Jenna found herself walking along the footpath back to her place admiring the trees dotted along the roadside. Jenna loved autumn, and spring the most out of all the seasons. The two seasons that were not in any way extreme or definitive. They had a good mix of weather, colour, and expectation about them and Jenna never did do extremes well in any situation. Life had taught her that. Adam's death and subsequent revelations about his second family confirmed it as had other events

over the years. Fortunately for Jenna
these events were arriving in her thoughts
less often now and with less emotional
intensity. Forgiveness had played a part
in all that, and Jenna had come to respect
that forgiveness in and of itself was a
process. There were no shortcuts to
anything in life Jenna had learned and it
was with this thought Jenna realised she
had walked right passed her place.
Turning around to head back she saw a
person waving to her. It must be Anne
she thought and walked up to her.

"I thought it was you. Going for
your morning walk?"

"No. It's a bit embarrassing really. I
have just been to see Dorothy and was
walking back, and got lost in my thoughts
and walked right passed my place."

"Let's be honest Jenna. You are
always getting yourself lost in your
thoughts. That's what makes you a
writer. I have some news. Do you have
time for a coffee?"

"I always have time for news Anne
as you know, and if coffee is on offer as
well? It is what one calls a win, win
situation." Jenna said and they both
smiled.

Anne made the coffee and took it through to the conservatory where she had directed Jenna to go. She retreated as quickly as she had set the coffee down returning with some small homemade lemon curd tarts.

"It has been years since I have seen those. My grandmother used to make them."

"My mother used her grandmother's recipe, and I came across her old cookbook last week when I was going through boxes in the spare room and put it to one side. They used quite different ingredients for cooking back then. Suet. Lard, and it surprised me that we can still get those things today. They are not as prominent of course but they do the trick. Anyway I was reading through it and came across this recipe and it brought back so many good memories. Oh Jenna I don't have the time to tell you of them all, but birthdays and Christmas they were always on the table, and they went with us on summer picnics, and to family gatherings. I am rambling." Anne said.

"Reminiscing, and from what I hear reminiscing is good for the soul." Jenna said.

"That's a very Scottish saying. Where did you hear that?" Anne asked.

"My grandfather was Scottish" Jenna told her.

"Anyway I decided I would have a go at making them, now eat up and tell me what you think."

Taking one off the plate and biting into it Jenna smiled and said "Absolutely delicious. Now what's this news I have come to hear?"

"I am going on a cruise, and wondered if you would be able to keep an eye on things while I'm away and take the treat bags to the rest home. I decided I may as well finish them even though Graham never made it that far.   I leave in two weeks. I will be spending Christmas on the high seas." Anne said with a smile.

"Are you going with a group?"

"No. My school friend Louisa and a friend are booked on the cruise. They had booked a cabin each, and the friend is not able to go, so I have been asked to go instead. I said I would think about it and let her know, then five minutes later I phoned her back and said yes. She has been busy informing the cruise ship people, I have paid the friend, my passport is all up to date, the airline tickets have been changed over, I have my travel insurance sorted, and I am driving to her place in Auckland the day before we leave. Everything Jenna has just fallen into place."

"I am so pleased for you."

"Do you know the best part Jenna? The very best part of all this, is that I don't have to ask permission to go. I just got to decide. Just like that. I made the decision and I get to enjoy the reward. No time to over think any of it. Do you know Jenna I am quite excited, and if I am honest it has been a very long time since I have been excited by anything at all?"

Observing Anne's body language, her relaxed face, and her hands being used expressively throughout the conversation Jenna was surprised by the thought that she had never seen Anne excited period, and what a transformation. She may have been excited by the upcoming cruise that had fallen into her lap, but it was more than that, Anne looked alive.

Neither of them had mentioned how soon it was to the passing of her husband Graham, and Jenna who was going to

bring that point up, thought better of it so
the words were left unuttered.

CHAPTER TWENTY

Jenna went over to Anne's the morning of her departure and collected the keys and Christmas treat bags for the rest home from her.

"I will water your plants indoors and the garden of course. The water restrictions will be in place, but they will get a regular dink don't worry about that. And I will clear your mail daily. Thank you for this." Jenna said as Anne handed her the contact information if she needed her urgently.

"Let's hope this time you don't need to contact me at all."

"I am not intending to contact you. I want you to have a fabulous time, and if you want to contact me you have my email address, and they will have Skype available no doubt, or something of that nature, but the truth of it is that you will be way too busy to be contacting anyone. Safe travels." Jenna said waving to Anne as she walked down the driveway.

It was December the fourth and Jenna was at the Christmas morning tea with the 'Coffin Club' group. Tania had arrived with some additional 'just in case books', and Jenna was signing copies for the members who were there, when another group of people arrived with books and money to buy more books, and to have them signed as well, and Jenna found herself quite taken aback.

It seemed word had got around and this created an issue not just for Jenna but for the group who were wanting to have their Christmas break-up morning tea.

When the people had left Jenna found herself giving a speech which began with "I am so very sorry. The book signing wasn't meant to become an event. Now let's get on with the reason we are here, and I would like to thank you all for the way you rallied and helped Jean get her husband's coffin ready. Jean is looking into setting up a group in her new community so she will be on the phone for advice and information over the coming months I am sure. Now let's eat, drink, and be grateful for all we have been blessed with." Jenna said.

Pam caught up with her once the group were all fed, and had their drink of choice.

"It is our fault Jenna that people turned up. I must say I was surprised by how many. Just how successful are you?"

"Very." Tania said. "And I am trying to get another book out of her. Honestly it is like pulling teeth."

"Well you know with the right instruments that never seems to be a problem." Pam said with a smile.

"Today is not about me." Jenna said sternly.

"Well it should be." Pam said. "You underestimate your own value Jenna. All these people, have come through or are still going through a process, in a much more healthy way, than they would have without your programme."

"It is not my programme." Jenna said.

"You put the money up front for the programme, and if you hadn't we would not have secured the funding to keep us going. Now that is an achievement Jenna

Mitchell and no doubt you apply the same diligence to your writing." Pam said in quite the no nonsense tone that she was known for, but that Jenna had never heard before.

Tania laughed, "I think Pamela would make a great publisher Jenna she has that mind-set."

"I think you two arranged that book signing between you to bully me into writing another book."

"Well she did phone me for additional books and invite me along."

"Now the truth comes out."

"Jenna I would never gate crash something in your personal life. I did say we should tell you but Pamela said there would only be a few."

"I am thinking about another book. I am just stuck on what to write about. It will come to me. I won't be starting work on it until April or May next year though."

"Okay Jenna that is good enough for me." Tania said helping herself to another Christmas mince pie.

Jenna had uncharacteristically accepted other invitations over the Christmas Season which gave her lots to talk about with Jean on their weekly catch-ups. The two church groups Jean had been more actively involved with than Jenna when she lived in the town, and the local gardening club Jenna had supported when she read about their need in the local paper for funds for two new glasshouses, now known as tunnel or green houses, depending on the materials they were constructed with.

So December was quite a full month with something scheduled in every week. Jenna put her past-time of browsing in the shops on hold after December the sixteenth as there were a lot more people in those shops. Stressed people Jenna thought as she watched their furrowed brows, their harsh tones, and rushed movements.

Jenna had got herself organised for Christmas much earlier this year, and as she had much less to do this year, the lead up to Christmas was a more enjoyable one than Jenna had thought it would be, or had been used to.

It was normally Jenna who was rushing around, with the harsh tone, furrowed brow and rushed movements. I could get used to this more laid back approach to Christmas she thought as she made her way to the supermarket to get her weekly stores in.

Jenna had found that being very early or much later in the day to be the optimal grocery shopping times at this time of the year.

The Christmas cake, nuts, mince pies, hams, Christmas cookies were all out on display and where are they hiding the Christmas puddings? Having found them in two places in the store Jenna decided on getting two small traditional plum puddings. One for her and one for Jean. Jenna also got two small and one large iced Christmas cakes, three packets of Christmas mince pies, three Christmas cookies, four packets of Christmas serviettes, some fresh meat and vegetables, dish wash and toilet paper.

The toilet paper made her smile "You always know how much more important you are when you sit upon the throne and realise you use toilet paper the same as everyone else." Her grandfather would say, and her grandmother if she was in ear shot would add "It comes down to the ply. One, two or three. No matter how stretched we have been your seat has been wiped with the first class variety."

Funny what the mind recalls Jenna thought, making her way to the checkout.

After Jenna had put away her groceries she set about making up the Christmas packs she had purchased the treats for.

One small iced cake, cookie, and packet of mince pies, with a packet of serviettes for Dorothy and the same for Jean with the addition of the Plum pudding. The large iced cake, one packet of mince pies and one cookie, with one packet of serviettes for Eden and Jason. Jenna had boxes for these items to go into and had made a Christmas Cookie Card for Jason's cookie to go into. Fresh fruit would be added to the box for Eden and Jason the day before Christmas to finish their gift off.

Yes Christmas was a time of giving and receiving and not for the first time, Jenna felt truly blessed long before she had received any Christmas gifts at all.

Jenna was at the supermarket first thing on Christmas Eve morning to purchase cherries, apricots and strawberries to go into her Christmas box for Eden and Jason, and while there she also purchased some chocolates to add.

They had boxes on special so Jenna bought three. Her calculation was that she was getting the three boxes for the same price as two with their normal pricing so why not. Why not indeed?

A very large box had arrived from overseas from her family in Australia, and there was a voucher waiting for Jenna to spend while she was in Canada the following year.

Jean phoned early that afternoon and assured Jenna, "I have not opened my parcel from you Jenna and that was very naughty of you." Sounding very pleased all the same. "Cyril and Joy were surprised you sent them something as well."

"You are most welcome. Enjoy. I will phone you on Boxing Day or are you busy?"

"Boxing Day would be lovely." Jean said.

At four o'clock that afternoon as previously arranged the Skype call from Stephanie and Richard came in, and Jenna was struck by how much they all chattered. What was particularly surprising to Jenna was how much of the chatter was done by Richard. David and

Deanna exchanged a few words with Jenna as well and just before the call had ended David said "Don't go to bed too early tonight mum we need to catch up with you when the munchkins are in bed." Jenna thought that may be easier said than done. If you only knew how often I doze off prior to going to bed these days, so she determined upon a course of action. Walking across to her DVD collection she decided on watching an action movie, with the fervent hope that it would keep her awake long enough to hear and respond to the call coming in from them.

Jenna busied herself with making her salad for dinner to join her lamb chop that was to be cooked in the frying pan on her stove top. One of her favourite CD's was playing in the background and dinner was served promptly at six o'clock.

Oh how Jenna remembered her father being a stickler for dinner promptly at six o'clock. Why it was six o'clock Jenna didn't know, but he had said it was tradition. Whose tradition he had never specified or explained, but it was to become their tradition none the less like it or lump it.

The great thing Jenna thought as she was enjoying her rather plump lamb chop is that traditions can be changed, and Jenna had set about changing the dinner time to work around her and her family which had meant over the years rather fluid eating timetables. At the end of the day everyone ate and on the weekends for at least two meals everyone ate together, and the shared time together was the most important part of the meal.

When the children had all left home meal times became a distant memory with Adam busy working all hours and being away. Jenna was often alone at meal times, in fact it was fairer to say Jenna was alone at meal times. These thoughts were thankfully interrupted by the doodoodoo….daadaadaa, and Jenna making her way to her computer to answer the call, and to her delight and surprise Karla and Bryce were smiling and saying "happy Christmas. We couldn't wait until tomorrow morning." Jenna who had been completely kept in the dark about the impromptu change in Bryce's work schedule was thrilled that all had worked out for good. The siblings in Australia had after all managed to spend

Christmas together and Jenna was very pleased for them all. David came on the call and said "I suppose you are feeling a bit left out now?"

"Not at all. I am pleased you are all together. We will be together soon enough. Karla is looking well."

"Karla is being swamped by Steph. You know how she adores her Aunt."

"So what did you want to talk to me about or was that a ruse?"

"No ruse. Just wait a moment I will get Deanna....Right perhaps this will be better coming from Deanna."

"It would seem you are to be a grandmother again. We haven't told the munchkins yet. We are barely getting to grips with it ourselves, but there you are."

"I thought you'd finished." Jenna said reacting to the news without thinking first.

"Yes well so had we, but nature has had another idea it would seem." Deanna said.

"I will make sure we mitigate any further surprises with a more permanent solution." David added.

"How are you both feeling about it?" Jenna asked them.

"Shocked and surprised and excited and annoyed all at once. Annoyed because we had hoped to be travelling in another five or six years. That was the plan. Not enrolling a child at the local school. But as you say plans change and we must learn to make the best of them. We wanted you to be the first to know." David said.

"So not ecstatic then?" Jenna voiced her observation of the two of them.

"It just seems so unfair. Karla and Bryce have been trying for ages and they haven't managed to get pregnant yet. Do we tell them now, after Christmas, when they get home, and there is Brittany and Vincent."

"Brittany and Vincent knew they were never going to have children of their own and they have made choices that fit their lives. Karla and Bryce, are trying and when the time is right for them it will happen, and if it's doesn't there is nothing they, you or I can do about it. They may very well look at other options. Deanna are you all right with this?" Jenna asked.

"Yes I think I am. I will be able to do all the wrong things right, and all the right things better, and of course we will have babysitters at the ready or easily accessed. We are older, but we are also better off financially, and I can take leave to be at home for the first twelve months so we will manage." And after a few more pleasantries were exchanged the call ended.

Jenna didn't know what to make of it all, but she knew that whatever gender arrived it would be loved like his or her two siblings had been. Yes David and Deanna were older but then, they had had their children early by today's standards, whereas like Karla a lot of women were starting their families later in life.

And then as if she had been hit by lightning Jenna knew why she had been so tired, puffy, agitated, hot and cold. She was at the end of her reproductive cycle. So as it should be she thought, the cycles carry on regardless of who you are, or where you find yourself in them. Not all things can be controlled by people all the time she thought, and found that quite comforting.

Making her way to the DVD player Jenna put the movie in, and went over to the table and tidied it off while the credits were rolling. Having made a cup of relaxing tea, she took that with her into the lounge, sat down and relaxed, watching the movie the evening taken care of.

The following Christmas morning Jenna was putting the final touches to the Hamper for Eden and Jason adding the fruit and chocolates to it when the computer started the now familiar Skype ring. Jenna answered the call and instead of Stephanie and Richard wishing her a Merry Christmas she was once again looking at Karla and Bryce. "We wanted to give you a special Christmas present this year. We are having a baby." Karla said with a beam from ear to ear, and Bryce had one to match. "We were going to tell you last night, but Karla thought it would be better to wait until this morning." Bryce said.

"I am thrilled for you both." Jenna said as they moved away and let Stephanie and Richard have the next round of Christmas cheer. After all their presents had been discussed Stephanie asked "have you opened our present yet?"

"Of course not. You know Steph I always wait for you to be present, now let me see." Said Jenna pulling their box nearer to her and opening the paper up, then using scissors to get through the tape holding the box together, before the present was revealed.

"I absolutely love it." Jenna said looking at the hand blown glass sculpture.

"I have just the right spot for it, and a table for it to sit on. It will give my foyer a new lease on life." Jenna said. "We are very pleased you like it." David said as he and Deanna came in to view. The others had moved into the lounge when Deanna said "Isn't it great news. We are so excited for them. They are over the moon."

"Yes I can see that." Jenna said.

"We thought we would keep the news of our new arrival to ourselves until they have gone home."

"That Deanna is very thoughtful."

"Well your first baby is the beginning of firsts for a lot of things isn't it? Say hi to Jason and his mum from us." Deanna said.

"We will be talking with Vincent and Brittany ten o'clock our time." David said before ending the call.

It always amused Jenna that when David was on a call of any kind to any one he just ended the call. It never occurred to him to ask if there was anything else. He was done so that was it. That was his father all over. Jenna thought and shook her head.

With the Hamper in the car, the house locked up, the glass sculpture in place from both the families living in Australia, Jenna started the car and made her way to Eden and Jason.

They had festive decorations on the front lawn complete with Christmas lights along the small driveway and the house was aglow with ornamentation. Jenna was quite taken aback.

Jason smiled. "I have been collecting some each year for my first proper Christmas home with Mum again." He said. "And I have something to tell you." He was saying as Jenna interrupted him "I'm sure you do, but please can you take this from me?" Jenna asked as she began off-loading the Hamper to him. "That's better. Either my arms are not as strong or I have put more in there than I intended. Sadly for you I think it is option one." Jenna said as Eden appeared, "has he told you yet. He has been itching to call you since he came home."

"No not yet. Merry Christmas Eden." Jenna said.

"Is this for us? Oh Jenna you shouldn't have."

"It's my pleasure. I know the appetite this one has," Jenna said putting her arm around Jason, "and there is a little something in there for you." She said.

"A Christmas cookie? Thank you. Now I can't wait any longer. I have been offered a job. An internship actually. I will be able to work and do my Master's at the same time. All paid for, oh and best of all. Mum can come over and live there with me if she wants, the package comes with an apartment and a car."

"Really? For all of that, you must be on track to finish your degree with Honours?"

"Yes Jenna. Just like I said I would. What I didn't expect was to be approached the way I was with the offer that came with them. It's very humbling you know. All the people out looking for work and a job like that has come to me."

"Well I would say well deserved and congratulations Jason. You really are a member of my family now. Another one living abroad permanently. I don't know how I do it." Jenna said and they all laughed.

After the lunch had been eaten and the trimmings cleared away Jason went around to see one of his school mates who had gone into the Army and was home on leave. Jenna was going to leave as well when Eden said. "There is no need for you to leave just yet Jenna. Come sit with me in the garden would you?"

Jenna was surprised at how enchanting the garden was for such a small space. It had a very homely feel to it. Sitting on the small chairs next to a small round table Jenna asked. "Are you going to shift to America to be with Jason?"

"To be honest Jenna I don't know. I have my work here, and I have a life here that I am happy with. The reality is Jason will go back, and I will go over from time to time and the bonus now is that we won't have the cost of accommodation. It seems to be that Jason's life is there for the moment as mine is here. I will see. When he left he never intended to live and work there."

"I know, but they take the best and that Eden is what you have raised. The best. Well done you."

"He had your help when he needed it."

"Fate is a wonderful thing Eden. It's all in the timing and the timing worked out well for all of us didn't it?"

"Yes I suppose it did." Eden replied and the two of them sat talking like long lost friends when Eden said "Oh my I nearly forgot. There is a present here for you Jenna. I will get it for you right now."

"But you have already given me a present." Jenna said.

Returning with a large bouquet of flowers Eden said. "Jean arranged for these to be delivered here yesterday so you would have flowers on Christmas Day, and she knew you would be here to receive them. Now where is it? Oh here it is. It had slipped down." She said handing Jenna the card which Jenna read out, "Have a fabulous Christmas Day from Cyril and the two Jays looking forward to January."

"Oh my goodness I wasn't expecting that." Said Jenna, "I am so pleased I sent a gift to Cyril and Joy."

I will put these on the table for you won't be a moment, and she wasn't. In no time at all she was back and asking "So what are you up to in January?"

It was late afternoon when Jenna arrived home. She put her bouquet of flowers in her mother's crystal vase, and the gift she had received from Jason and Eden, a lovely pamper gift that found a home in her bathroom before doing the check on Anne's house where all seemed to be in order.

On her return home she made herself a cup of orange tea and reflected on what an absolutely delightful Christmas day it had been, and like an infomercial she reminded herself but wait there's more, and there was. Christmas would not be complete until she had spoken with Vincent, Brittany and her parents.

Jenna kept herself busy until the call arrived and as she had expected it was lovely talking with them all. The call lasted a good twenty minutes, "Just so you know. Karla and Bryce are with your brother so that will be just the one call to them."

"So how are they?" Vincent asked.

"If I tell you that there wouldn't be much point in your calling them now would there?" Jenna said.

"Such a man. I told you." Brittany said with her father calling out "Steady on you." And then all too quickly the call ended. Jenna looked over at her clock and realised it was later than she thought so she decided to go to bed.

Lying on the new lush feather down pillows she had bought for herself this Christmas Jenna closed her eyes feeling loved, grateful and very blessed, and not once that whole day had she felt alone.

Ends

About The Author

KAREN PIVOTT is the author of Self Help, Children's and Adult Fiction books, *and is a published radio scriptwriter with HCJB Beyond the Call with Ron Cline series 2001. Radio Southland 2004 and 2005.* Published play write "Gavin's 21st." 2000 Nelson fringe art festival and literacy specialist. Karen lives in Invercargill New Zealand with her husband. Karen loves educating and inspiring people to improve their lives and the lives of all the people they connect with.

Karen has a Facebook page "It Starts With You" where she has inspirational quotes and a weekly blog of challenges and tips to enhance the lives of her readers.

https://www.amazon.com/author/karenpivott

Copyright © 2017 Karen Pivott

All Rights Reserved

www.ingramcontent.com/pod-product-compliance
Lightning Source LLC
Chambersburg PA
CBHW051045050726
47592CB00002B/393